Whom You Will Serve

DICK DERKSEN

 **FriesenPress**

One Printers Way
Altona, MB R0G 0B0
Canada

www.friesenpress.com

Copyright © 2021 by Dick Derksen
First Edition — 2021

Illustrations by Jeraldine Derksen

All rights reserved.

No part of this publication may be reproduced in any form, or by any means, electronic or mechanical, including photocopying, recording, or any information browsing, storage, or retrieval system, without permission in writing from FriesenPress.

ISBN
978-1-03-911956-7 (Hardcover)
978-1-03-911955-0 (Paperback)
978-1-03-911957-4 (eBook)

1. FICTION, AMISH & MENNONITE

Distributed to the trade by The Ingram Book Company

The History Lesson: Prologue

The major event of the 17th Century in northern Europe is the Thirty Years War, lasting from 1618-48, and involving much of northern Europe in a sectarian war with huge political implications. The events of this book cover only a small portion of this war, with only those principalities involved that likely affected the Derksen family. The Mennonites had found refuge in Wuestenfelde on the Fresenburg Estate in the sixteenth century, which is the scene of Book 1 *Choose You This Day*, but within seventy years of the activities of that first book in this series, they hear that the safety of their home is threatened once again. Since early in the 17th Century, Mennonites had found refuge in several locations across northern Europe, one of which is a village adjoining the Hanseatic city of Hamburg. At the time of this volume, Altona is a town that is rapidly becoming a small city, as refugees of all kinds joined the industrious citizens of this community.

Altona is situated within Holstein, thus ruled by Christian IV of Denmark, who is also Duke of Holstein and an Elector of the Holy Roman Empire. He is a Protestant, a Lutheran, protecting Protestants against the combined imperial armies of Baron Johann von Tilly and Albrecht von Wallenstein. He enters the war against the Catholic

1

imperialists, when the Catholics win the Battle of White Mountain in Bohemia against the Protestant forces of Frederick V, King of Bohemia. His army is defeated in 1626 by the combined forces of Tilly and Wallenstein, who then occupy Holstein and root out places where Protestants live, including Wuestenfelde, the village where Menno Simon lived the last years of his life. We do not read any more at this time about Baron von Ahlefeld, so we must assume that his family line had ceased, and he had passed his control over the Fresenburg Estate to Christian IV. Between 1627 and 1629, Wuestenfelde is leveled to the ground by Tilly and Wallenstein, leaving the location of a great deal of Mennonite history totally obliterated. Great hardships and dangers are faced by the fleeing Mennonites, who once more become refugees from greater religious powers around them, their pacifistic beliefs preventing them from protecting their homes and families. Altona becomes their next refuge, still officially under the protection of Christian IV of Denmark, Duke of Holstein, administered by the Counts von Schauenburg, but riding in the shadow of the large industrial city of Hamburg, which also accepts Mennonite refugees, but with more restrictions. Cities that have joined the League of Hansa, such as Hamburg, Bremen, Luebeck and Danzig, are independent of the Emperor and also independent of the princes that ruled the territories surrounding them. Their government is normally an oligarchy of wealthy merchants, protecting mostly their own interests. In Altona and Hamburg the Mennonites forge a new life for themselves as town and city dwellers.

A parallel story is unfolding at the same time as this one, but in a different part of Europe and with a different offshoot of the Anabaptist movement from which the Mennonites had sprung. The Hutterian Brethren had moved from Tyrol during the time when George Blaurock, a colleague of Felix Manx and Conrad Grebel in the Anabaptist movement in Zurich, Switzerland, under Zwingli in 1525, had moved to Nikolsburg in Moravia, just north of Vienna, and were protected by the Lords von Liechtenstein, who ruled that area. One of them was actually baptized into the Anabaptist movement. The years from 1565-92 were the Golden Years for Moravian Hutterites. The idea of community of goods was practiced, largely following the example of the first church in Acts chapter 2, but also as a practical way to live in a state of refuge in a strange new world. A large group broke off the main group, led by Jacob Wiedemann, and moved to Austerlitz, a deserted village nearby. In 1621, Prince Gabor Bethlen of Transylvania kidnapped 85 Hutterites from Moravia, treated them well, and saw 800 more join them in Romania. For a time, community of goods was abandoned, as each family sought refuge from persecution wherever it could, when the Austro-Hungarian monarch rooted them out.

During the Thirty Years War, in 1622, Cardinal von Dietrichstein expelled the Hutterites, who had followed Jacob Hutter following the death of George Blaurock, from Moravia, so they moved to Slovakia. Hutterite communities became prime targets for plundering, burning and looting.

Two hunred seventy-five Lutherans from Carinthia, Austria, joined them in 1755, bringing a miraculous spiritual revival. Because they were impressed with the teachings of the Hutterite leaders, they established several new communities of goods, reviving the old order. Some sixty or seventy decided to move to Russia when Empress Maria Theresia sought to stamp out heresy in her realm in 1762, arriving in Vishenka, northeast of Kiev; then, in 1796, they moved farther to Radichev, where suffering brought about abandonment of community of goods once again. Spiritual bankruptcy had once again set in. Faced with economic ruin, they appealed to Johann Cornies, the agricultural pioneer from the Mennonite Molotschna Colony, for help. They established Huttertal, learned modern farming techniques from Cornies, improved their educational standards, and, in 1852 established Johannesruh in honour of Johann Cornies. Since this takes us into several books from this one, we'll leave the story there for now, but incorporate what we can into this one.

Dick Derksen

The Bubonic Plague still tends to rear its head, particularly following military interventions. Normal functions of life, such as childbirth, take a high toll on Mennonites, as well as society in general. Medicine is still at a very primitive state, though new diagnostic tools are constantly being introduced, one of the greatest of these being the microscope. Laws are constantly tightened, to make life more difficult for the Dissenters. Dissention comes easily in such a close-knit interdependent community, and the Mennonites are not spared. Group forms against group, citing rival scripture texts as proof of their own validity. Personal pressures become so great that nerves sometimes become fragmented.

Gerritt Roosen, an actual person who was about 16 years old at the time of this story, is introduced, but he was later both a successful hosiery merchant and a preacher in the Mennonite church for fifty years, dying a few months short of 100 years old in 1711, and he is noted for his guidance of the church through several disputes, some of which I have introduced prematurely in this story. In spite of every obstacle, the Mennonite community forges a new life in strange surroundings. In the end, however, many feel that the pressures of city life make it too difficult to live out their beliefs, and they plan to move further east to join others that have found refuge in West Prussia. I have anticipated the next volume in this series with these plans.

I should say a word about my spellings of terms in Plautdietsch and High German: I have adopted the equivalent High German spelling for the sounds of the dialect. That is contrary to how many 'Russian Mennonites' in Canada and USA spell their writings, where an Anglicized spelling is preferred. Because I lived in Germany for so long, my High German is much better than my Plautdietsch, so I drift naturally into how the Germans would spell their dialect terms. I have avoided the use of the Umlaut, which is two dots above the letter, as it presents reading problems for those not introduced to its use. Instead I have substituted, as Germans also do, the affected vowel plus an 'e' to indicate where the vowel would normally have an Umlaut. The function of the Umlaut is to change the pronunciation of the vowel. The reader will also note that in German, all nouns are capitalized, except adjectival nouns. German vowels are normally straight, that is, they follow what we in the choral world call 'Italian vowels', where we sing ah, ay, ee, oh, uh, instead of the English ay, ee, eye, oh, you. When these sounds differ from the open vowel, the Umlaut is used to indicate that change of sound, so the ah (letter "a" in English) sound diverts to ae, which is pronounced like the ai in 'said', but with the lips pulled inwards from the sides. The Umlaut is used primarily with a, o and u, which in my text renders them ae, oe and ue. Another Germanism is the fact that ei is pronounced like 'eye' in English, while ie is pronounced like 'ee'. Consonants, such as W and J also have different pronunciations from the English equivalents. "W" is pronounced as a V would be in English, and "J" is pronounced as Y in the word you.

I am Richard John (Dick) Derksen, born November 22, 1939, in Lowe Farm, Manitoba. Moved in October 1947 to Mission, BC, and in May, 1952, to Vanderhoof, BC. I am the eldest of fifteen children. After a disastrous house fire that destroyed almost everything our family owned, I had to quit attending one-room country school after Grade 8. To help with family finances I worked in my father's sawmill and small farm until I was almost 21, taking my ninth grade by BC Correspondence after work each evening. I then went to Prairie Bible Institute for four years, graduating in 1964, after which I went back to Prairie and finished high school there in 1966. In my years at Prairie, I also worked off an apprenticeship in barbering by doing gratis work in the institutional barber shop and received my Alberta Trades License in the fall of 1964. After a summer as Assistant Director at Ness Lake Bible Camp near Prince George, BC, I moved to Calgary in September, 1966 and entered the B.Ed. program at University of Calgary, majoring in school music.

I married Jeraldine Joy (Jerry) Wilkinson, a former classmate at PBI on August 31, 1968, in the middle of my B.Ed. studies. I finished university in 1970, while Jerry worked as an operating-room nurse and I worked in barber shops and construction. I taught junior high in Calgary for six years while also directing Whispering Pines Bible Camp. Two sons, Derek Richard (1971) and Devon Gerald (1973), were born to us during this time. Jerry's hobbies include drawing and painting. She is the artist for the illustrations in this book. The rest of my introduction will follow in Volume 5, as I develop the story of the Mennonites into my own generation and my own autobiography.

Geneology of the Derksen Family

As created by Dick Derksen, 2010 to 2021
Fictional at This Stage, but Possible

Jacob	Age	Places Lived	Details	Children	Occupation
Jacob Derksen I	1505-1580	Witmarsum, various, Muenster, Witmarsum, Wuestenfelde	Converted to Mennism over a period of time around 1536, along with Menno Simon. Married to Eva; eight children, of whom 5 survive to adulthood.	~~Henry~~ Leah Jake Aron Frederic ~~Isaac~~ Sarah ~~Miriam~~ ~~(Schaetzli)~~ +	Mason, Deacon in Mennonite Church, Built barns for Baron Bartholomew von Ahlefeld
Jacob II (Jake)	1536-1627	Wuestenfelde, Bad Oldesloe, Altona	With the martyr-dom of Henry, Jake becomes the oldest male, second to Leah, who is a year older. Jake marries Heidi, has one son, Jacob III.		Carpentry in the Baron's shop, deacon in Mennonite Church

7

Dick Derksen

| Jacob III | 1581-1656 | Wuestenfelde, Altona | Born after years of barrenness, married to Rebekah Thiessen, by whom five children are born. Rebekah dies in delivery of Jacob IV (JJ). They take in five Guenther children, whose parents die of the Plague. Marries the widow Martina Roosen, but the unconsummated marriage is annulled; then he marries his cousin Dorcas, daughter of Leah and Heinrich Gerbrandt, his father's sister. Five children with Rebekah, two with Dorcas; sort of adopted the two Roosen children. Planning to move to Heubuden, Royal Prussia, but thwarted. | Benjamin Joshua Mary Elizabeth Jacob IV Guenther Children Susan Nickolas Jonathan Agnes Willy Roosen Children Gerritt Lizzy Children by Dorcas Heinrich Jacob Heidi Leah | Carpentry in the Baron's shop; preacher in Mennonite Church, Manager of Mennonite Manufacturing (wagons, ironware) Elder in the Mennonite district |

Chapter 1

"The Catholics are coming! The Catholics are coming!" The shrill voice of the messenger rang through the village street of Wuestenfelde. Mothers and children came out of their houses, surprised and anxious at the news. The men were mostly at work, either in the various shops on the Fresenburg Estate, or on their own small fields. The messenger did not remain anywhere long, but kept up his loud cries before every house until he was at the end of the village. Mothers quickly sent children to find their fathers and to pass on the news to them. They, if they worked in one of the shops, had already heard and were on their way to their houses. Those in the fields could only be informed by their children and make whatever speed they could to their families.

Christian IV, Lutheran King of Denmark and Duke of Holstein, had lost several important battles against the Catholic forces of the Holy Roman Emperor, led by Johann Tsaerelaes Count von Tilly, from Belgium, and the Austrian Albrecht Eusebius Wenzel von Wallenstein. Protestant Christians had been forced to withdraw from the war, giving the armies of the Catholic generals free reign in the area of Holstein controlled by him. It was in this northern German state that the

Mennonites had sought safety under Baron Bartholomew von Ahlefeld, owner of the Fresenburg Estate at Bad Oldesloe, and where the outlying village of Wuestenfelde provided shelter to the Mennonites.

Neither the armies of the Emperor nor of the Austrian warlord were paid, so they lived by plundering the areas that they had conquered. Any area predominantly settled by Protestants of any kind was especially picked for their immediate needs. Since Christian IV was a Lutheran, any part of Holstein was fair game, but since there were still Lutheran armies around, not all towns were attacked immediately. Heretic sects, such as the Mennonites, Hutterites and Amish, however, had been brutally removed from Bohemia a few years prior to this. Thus, Wuestenfelde was especially being targeted at this time.

"Benjamin, see if Father is coming," called Rebekah Derksen to her eldest son. At twelve, he was quite mature, and he obediently went out to the road and looked toward Bad Oldesloe, to see if he could spot his father coming down the road. He saw several men coming toward him, so it was difficult to determine exactly who was who, but finally he saw him come around the last bend. He rushed back to the house and calmed his mother with the news.

"Quick, everyone must pack everything of your own, just as you have been told before, because we must leave our house to the soldiers," commanded Rebekah to her children. Although some were not old enough to understand, somehow they sensed that it was important to look for things that meant something to them. Each one began looking for containers of any kind to pack things in. Father would be bringing the wagon with the horses around to the door between the house and the barn, so they could load their things. Because of the imminent danger, this had been rehearsed several times, and the children remained remarkably controlled in their emotions, though the tension was quite high. Father had set a number of things aside near this door, so that loading could be accomplished quite efficiently. Mother, too, had many things ready beforehand, to help with the inevitable move that they must undertake.

"The army is coming down from the northwest," Father indicated, as he began the loading process with his eldest son, "so it is best to go southward toward Hamburg. Most of the Mennonites are heading for Altona, just outside Hamburg, where other Mennonites have lived for generations. We'll go there, too, because we also have relatives there. Some have said that they are going to Luebeck, and I think they can make it past the army, too."

The Mennonites were well aware of the danger of the Catholic army coming their way, so all of them had discussed the impending departure in great detail, the leaders had outlined specific plans, in the event that an evacuation would have to be carried out. Soon an orderly train of wagons was seen departing toward Bad Oldesloe, through which they must travel on their way to Altona. The Derksen clan was among them.

The original Jacob Derksen that had come to Wuestenfelde just prior to Menno Simon's coming had left five living children, three of which were boys. Jake had married Heidi Hildebrand, and Aron and Frederic had also grown up, married and had families. The girls, Leah and Sarah, had married and had families. Leah and Heinrich Gerbrandt had twelve children, four of which had died in childbirth, and Sarah had married Samuel Voth, youngest son of Abe Voth, for whom Jake had worked, with whom she had four children. Jacob III, the only child of Jake and Heidi, and his wife Rebekah were now carrying the Jacob Derksen name to another location. Their family was comprised of Benjamin, twelve years old, Joshua, ten, Mary, nine, and Elizabeth, seven.

The year was 1627, and Jake and Heidi were now 91 years old and quite feeble. They too, had to be brought on the wagon to Altona. Jacob III – we'll call him Jacob, though he had been Jakie all of his growing up years – had a heavy load on the wagon, so Benjamin and Joshua, as well as Mary, had to walk behind the wagon. Rebekah and Elizabeth would also walk occasionally, particularly if the road was not too good, as the horses then had more work in pulling the wagon.

The wagon train had begun to travel in the late afternoon, so they were not able to make a great deal of progress before nightfall overtook them. Details of the advancing army were sketchy, but it was not expected that they were close enough to be an immediate threat. Besides, it had been noted that they were not in the habit of attacking fleeing villagers, even though they were Protestants or other sects. They seemed to be satisfied to take the villagers' livelihood, destroy their homes, and leave. That is what those in Bohemia had suffered, and that is what others in Holstein had suffered. In the years since 1554, when Jacob I and Eva had arrived in Wuestenfelde, they had acquired some means of subsistence. Their barn was full, and their crops were substantial. They had their own team of good draft horses, three cows with calves, five ewes with lambs and a ram, and about thirty laying hens and five roosters. Other Mennonites had fared similarly well. Now the third generation after them was transporting most of their worldly goods in wagons to start a new life in a small town alongside a large industrial, trading city. Most of the livestock had to be left behind to become food for the approaching army. Jacob was keeping his best milk cow, so she was tethered behind the wagon, leaving her calf trying to follow along and suckle as they moved.

A simple overnight bivouac was arranged, with everyone sleeping under the stars in their family groups. No special attention was given to security, as they did not expect the army to be pursuing them.

Early the next morning, a communal fire was built, over which a large pot hanging from an iron tripod was steaming with the odour of multi-grain porridge. Each one brought a bowl and one of the women ladled out the cereal. The group seemed to have grown overnight, as latecomers had joined those who had gotten an earlier start. Once everyone had eaten, the horses were brought from where they had been tethered on a grassy field, watered, harnessed and hitched back to the wagons, and the leaders began the move towards Altona.

Because the wagons were heavily loaded, and because livestock was being brought along, progress was somewhat slow, so another bivouac was made the following night. Parts of the road were deeply rutted and dirty puddles covered most of these parts. Jacob's wagon got stuck in one of the rutted puddles, and other teams were brought, along with long chains, to assist his team, which could no longer move the wagon through the quagmire. One chain snapped as the teams pulled, and a part flew and hit one of the horses on the back, which made it jump sideways and get the harness tangled. It took the men a full hour to get the horses back under control and find another chain. Eventually they got the wagon moving, but then the axle broke, and the whole load fell partially into the muddy water. One of the other wagons was hastily emptied and brought alongside the Derksens' broken one, so that the men could move everything from the broken one to the other. When that one had been brought to a drier spot, the men began to wade into the water once more to survey the damages to the axle and the rest of the wagon.

"We will have to make a new axle from one of the oak trees near the road," remarked Jacob. "I guess my carpentry training will have to help me out here on the road. I kept the crosscut saw and some other tools on my wagon here, in case we had to do something like that."

The men went scouting for suitable wood, taking the saw and axes with them. After about an hour, they returned, dragging a piece of the tree behind them. Jacob stood over it with a wide axe and began to shape the trunk roughly into an axle. Then he used the other tools to finish it, so that the wheel could be put back on. A hole had to be drilled through the wood at each end for the pin that held the wheel onto the axle. This took the longest, for drills were still somewhat primitive, and oak wood is very hard.

Next came the job of mounting the axle under the wagon. First the crippled vehicle had to be pulled out of the watery ruts to dry ground. That accomplished, the men set about removing the broken axle from under the wagon, using other pieces of wood as levers to raise the wagon. Wrenches did not want to turn the rusted nuts on the old bolts, but someone had an adjustable pipe wrench that would work. He went all the way to his wagon to fetch it, and came back panting. Finally the rusted nuts gave way, and the men were able to remove the old pieces of wood. Then the group took positions along both sides of the new axle and moved it into place. With a bit of grease from some bacon, the nuts went onto the bolts much easier, and soon the axle was solidly mounted under the wagon, with the wheels properly lined up. The team was hitched to the wagon once more, and everyone moved to where the goods were being kept dry. The Derksens' goods were loaded from the other wagon back onto theirs, and the other person's goods were loaded back onto his wagon, and several hours behind those who had gone on, the smaller group was able to begin once more.

The third day saw the front wagons enter Altona by mid-afternoon. The last ones, including the Derksens', creaked into the village at nearly midnight. No one had been hurt *en route*, and the Derksens' wagon had been the only one suffering damage. Horses and other livestock seemed to be in good condition, the lashing with the chain not having left any permanent damage. Women and children had all survived the trip without too much strain. Even Jake and Heidi were in fairly good spirits, in spite of the discomforts accorded them in their old age. Word had been sent ahead to Count Ernst von Schauenburg, under whose administration Altona lay, so military tents had been set up on a large open space to receive the refugees. A group of Mennonites from Altona had been appointed to oversee the settling in of the newcomers.

"Help, Suzie is gone." The shrill cry of Susan Dyck rang through the camp, rousing men and women to find out what had happened. "We can't find Suzie," the distraught woman cried out again. Her husband, Johann, was running thither and yon, looking behind every wagon and under everything that could hide a person, seeking his seventeen-year-old daughter. Suzie was arguably the prettiest girl among the Mennonites who had made the journey from Wuestenfelde to Altona. Her beauty had made her a bit self-conscious of what she could do to the young men, and everyone suspected the worst. The men organized themselves into brigades, found items that could serve as torches, and began to comb the area around the camp, then spread out into an ever wider circle, searching everywhere that a person might be hiding, or might be lying. Meanwhile, Jonathan and Susan Dyck tried to recall the last time they had seen their daughter. It seemed to them that it had been shortly after dark, when she was seen with a group of the Mennonite young people on the edge of the camp. But, the young people were now with their families, and none could remember where Suzie had gone after they had been together, as they had all gone directly to their wagons.

The men searched as diligently as they could, but Suzie could not be found. Disappointed, they returned to the camp. By now it was nearing 2:00 AM, and they had had a long hard day on the road. They decided, much against the wishes of Jonathan and Susan, to call off the search and hope that Suzie would return on her own.

Next morning, while a few men continued the search, others were busy about the camp. A community kitchen was organized to prepare food for the group, which numbered well over a hundred people, and capable people took over the cooking, cleaning and other necessary chores. Men went for firewood and water, taking turns with their wagons. Soon a wholesome breakfast could be smelled from the farthest wagons in the camp, bringing young and old for their portion. After breakfast the men got back to work on making the camp livable. Sanitation was arranged, so that within a couple of days, a routine of life was setting in.

Excitement mounted as a cry was heard from afar, "We found her!" Everyone rushed toward the street where the men were leading a shabby, disheveled girl back to camp. Jonathan and Susan rushed ahead of everyone else to welcome their returning daughter. But, to their dismay, Suzie tried to shoo them away. She appeared not to want to come to her own parents. They, of course, could not understand what would motivate her to alienate herself from her closest family. When the parents wouldn't give up trying to come near her, she cried out, "He raped me!" As the truth began to dawn on her parents and on the rest of the community, who had been so joyful to see her coming back into the camp, they began to lower their gaze in thoughtful silence. The men gave her over to Jonathan and Susan to console and comfort, while they reported to George Toews, their Schultze, or leader.

George called the council together, made up of leading men in the Mennonite community, and the council served both as the civil government and the church deacons' board. There was no distinction made between civil matters and religious matters. Everything was naturally integrated in a Mennonite's mind.

"Men, we have had something terrible happen to our community," George began. Jacob was one of the council members, and he agreed with his whole spirit. He could envision his own daughter, when she became that age, being taken by some unscrupulous man for his own pleasure. "We don't know who did this awful thing to one of our daughters, but we must find out. If it is one of the German boys from Altona or Hamburg, we can go to the magistrates about the matter, and they will take care of things according to their law. The question is going to be this: If it is one of our own boys, or more of them, what are we going to do with them?"

"We will castrate him," stated one of the men, boldly.

"We will hang him from the big Linde in the middle of our camp," stated another.

"Is that the way Menno taught us to treat someone who does something against us," asked Jacob. "Is that the way Jesus taught us to treat those who despitefully use us?" he continued.

There was deathly silence in the group. "Surely we aren't expected to love someone that does something like that to one of our daughters," the one that suggested taking the knife to the culprit stated plaintively, almost questioningly.

"Well, what do we believe the Bible teaches us in such a case?" Jacob, who was their leading preacher, somewhat of a pastor, asked. "Do we treat each other the same way the world around us treats their neighbor?"

"How do you treat a shameful, dangerous person in love?" asked another council member.

"God punishes sin, so we must also punish it. This is certainly sin," stated another with finality.

"If we are to treat him in love, then, we spare his life. Therefore, castration is a loving response to the criminal," stated the advocate again, quite forcefully this time.

Just then, the meeting was interrupted, as a magistrate from Altona entered the room. He looked around at the group, and seeing George, he went over to him and whispered something in his ear. George nodded, looked at the man, and thanked him for coming. He then promptly left the room.

"Gentlemen, I am happy to inform you that we won't have to deal with the situation further. The policemen have apprehended one of the young men from Altona, who was identified by Suzie as the one who molested her," George said. The men expressed surprise that the guilty one had been found that soon. They were even more surprised that Suzie had been willing to identify him. Jonathan, her father, was also a council member, but he was understandably absent from this meeting. Perhaps he had persuaded her to go with him to the police station. At any rate, the town magistrate had been satisfied that this was the guilty party, and he was now in the town jail, awaiting trial. What would be done with him was not known to the Mennonites, but they knew that the matter was now out of their hands.

Traders from Hamburg traveled through much of Holstein, and they were informed of where the army was located, what its plans were, and what damages were done to local farms and villages. Wuestenfelde, the group was told, had been completely destroyed. Not one building was left standing. Even monuments, such as Menno's grave, could no longer be found. Jacob, having taken over as village pastor from Jake, his father, called the group together and led them in a prayer of thankfulness for God's timely warning to them and His protection over them. In spite of their difficult situation, the group rejoiced that no one from the village had suffered direct threats from the army or been killed, and that God had led them to a new life in Altona and Luebeck. At the same time, Jacob prayed for the Dyck family, and especially for Suzie, that no permanent damage was done to her, and that the family could cope with this terrible thing. Even the Dycks went home encouraged.

Dick Derksen

Mennonite refugees in Altona

Chapter 2

"Rats!" word got around the camp rather quickly, but not quickly enough. A number of the sneaking rodents were seen entering baggage stored on the ground in and around tents. By this time it was suspected that rats carried the dreaded bubonic plague, and a general fear swept through the camp.

The men who were leaders in the group immediately got together to plan their strategy. It would not do to allow the creatures to remain among their possessions. Very soon one or another of them would get aggressive and bite someone who got too close.

"We must set up some traps to catch them," they agreed, and set about trying to find suitable traps that could be baited and set out during the night. The local town officials were more than helpful in locating such contraptions, and in suggesting suitable bait for them. They were soon set up in strategic locations throughout the camp.

"We have to try to get every rat out of our baggage, too," they surmised. "Has anyone got a good idea of how we might do that?" No one really wanted to dismantle every box and bag to find each and every rat, but that seemed the only way they would be sure. Where to store the baggage, so that rats wouldn't get into it again was the next question.

"What happens when we sleep on the ground and they get into bed with us?" another leader questioned. "Perhaps we should get our pastor to gather the group together for prayer, to ask God to protect us and our few remaining possessions," another suggested. That seemed good to all of them, as they could then also issue the warnings appropriate to the problem to everyone. One of them went to find Jacob III, to ask him to call another prayer meeting this evening.

Jacob agreed, and he suggested that his father, Jake, be asked to lead in this prayer of supplication. As the oldest member of the group, his prayer would be appreciated by everyone, and perhaps some would even attribute special grace to his prayers, because he had served them well for so many years as lay pastor, just as his only son was now doing. Word went out quickly, and after the evening meal, the whole camp joined together for a time of supplication, led by Jake Derksen and his son, Jacob. Afterwards, they all retired to their quarters, seeking to make their tents and possessions as rat proof as possible.

The leaders had been working tirelessly to find suitable housing for their people, but this was not easy, for Altona had been growing with other refugees migrating to the outskirts of the big city, and they had taken all the available houses and apartments. The town council members were approached about possible public housing that might be made available to the new settlers. It was apparent to all that this group was going to make Altona their new home, as their old home had been totally destroyed. There was nothing in Wuestenfelde to go back to, and nothing else at this time to look forward to. A few dwellings in Altona were found, but not enough for the whole group. Some would have to seek lodging in Hamburg or elsewhere in the area. Jewish refugees had gotten there from Spain and Portugal shortly before the Mennonites, and they had been given most of the available dwellings in Hamburg, as they were not allowed to farm or buy land. Several Mennonite farmers found places to rent outside the town, where they could continue their chosen occupation in relative peace. Because they had not been able to bring along their previous implements, they were forced to rent the places with their implements, which made the terms of their rental somewhat complicated. The Jews preferred to live in the city, so most of them moved downtown as soon as possible, and some Mennonites also began to make trips into Hamburg, to see what they could find. Jacob and Rebekah were among this group, as they needed a place where not only their immediate family could live, but also his aged parents, Jake and Heidi. In addition, Jacob, like his father, had learned the trade of carpentry, so he was looking for work in one of the many shops devoted to that occupation. After several days, a suitable house was found on the western side of the city, near Altona, and quite close to it, a shop that required a fine cabinet maker. The war, however, had diminished the orders drastically, so the workers were paid by the piece, as orders came in. Jacob was able to garner a few orders for basic cupboards and wardrobes from the Mennonites that had come with him, as well as from the Jews that had also drifted into the city at this time, and with that, he was able to get the family settled into its own house.

Jake and Heidi had a comfortable main-floor apartment with a separate entrance, so that they had a sense of being independent, but Rebekah and Jacob and their children could easily visit between the two parts of the house. The elderly ones were well cared for, and quite happy with this arrangement. Jacob and his family were also relatively comfortable, as they found creative ways to divide up the rooms for their various needs. There was even a room near the entrance that could be used as an office by the pastor part of Jacob, and a lean-to shed at the back that provided for the carpenter part of him, as well as for many other storage and practical uses. Their part of the house had numerous stairways. That took some getting used to, as their house in Wuestenfelde had been one of the usual house-barn combinations, with a loft above the house where the boys slept.

It was obvious that they would no longer need the draft horses that had brought them to Hamburg, so Jacob put them up for sale, along with the repaired wagon that had carried their goods. Unknown to him, the man that bought them was an agent of the Catholic army under

Wallenstein, and the rig became a transport vehicle for the opposition. The cash, however, was well invested in necessary items for their new home, and for a light horse and a carriage. The lean-to provided storage for the carriage and stabling for the horse and the cow. As things began to take shape around them, they were sitting in their living area in the evening, drinking a hot mulled wine, when Rebekah looked at Jacob with a winsome smile and said, "I think we are going to need a crib in about eight months." Jacob was astonished. Another child? He had thought that part of their life was behind them, their being in their late forties, and that they would simply enjoy the children God had given them. Would it be another boy, or a girl? Either was fine with him, so long as it was healthy. He got up from his chair, walked over to Rebekah and gave her a warm hug. Then they made themselves ready for bedtime.

Helping all the families to get settled took the next days, with a break for a Sunday morning worship service, at which Jacob preached. His father, Jake, preceded him with a greeting of his own, as well as a bit of church and family history.

"My father and mother, along with Menno Simon and his family and many others, fled Friesland when the Catholic Church began persecuting us for our faith. We wandered from place to place, seeking shelter and safety, but no one would risk taking us in, for fear of their own safety. Finally, Baron Bartholomew von Ahlefeld invited us to his Fresenburg Estate, which he had inherited in 1543. My father was a bricklayer who built the Baron's barns and many of the houses we lived in. Heidi took her Latin school in Luebeck, so that she could become the schoolteacher for our group in Wuestenfelde, and I took cabinet-making during our first year of marriage, as she finished her schooling. We returned to Wuestenfelde at the end of our studies and began to work in the community. Menno died shortly after that, and we had no pastor any more. Still, the Baron kept up his support for our group of Mennonites, so the community at Bad Oldesloe-Wuestenfelde prospered. My father was a deacon, as were some of your fathers, and they began to take turns preaching. Then, one day they asked whether I would preach. To make a long story short, I accepted, and I have been your pastor ever since, along with occasional work as a cabinet-maker. We had trouble having children, and it took a number of years before we had any. Finally, we had a son, our only child, who is now your pastor. He followed in my footsteps and learned the trade of cabinet-making. Our son, Jacob III, who has blessed us with four lovely grandchildren and tells me that there is a fifth one on the way – here there was an interruption, as the congregation expressed its surprise and congratulations – he has taken over from me as pastor when I could no longer carry on in that work, and I trust he is satisfactory to you all. Now that we have fled persecution again, and we don't know what God has in mind for our future, we need the guidance of someone who studies the Word of God and can make it practical to each one of us. We must not lose our faith, no matter what happens. God will save us. God will save us!"

At this, Jake's breath was coming in short, sharp gasps, so Jacob and one of the deacons escorted the feeble man back to his chair, which was padded with quilts to provide a bit of comfort. Heidi, who could hardly hear a word he had said, squeezed his arm as he sat down painfully beside her in the front row, beside the benches that had been set up in the large shed where church was being held. With that, Jacob returned to the makeshift pulpit to begin his sermon.

"Brethren and sisters, we live in perilous times," Jacob began. "It did not take long in what we thought would be a safe place, that someone took advantage of one of our own to commit sin on her. We also see that the enemies of God, who pose as messengers of God, attack those of us who seek a true relationship with God through faith alone in Jesus Christ." Jacob continued in this vein for some time, citing biblical references regarding those who would attack those of the true faith, and claiming that the present situation they found themselves in was a direct result of such persecution of God's true believers. He urged everyone to remain steadfast, in spite of hardships and dangers, and to hold on to the faith that they had claimed at their baptism. He reminded them that their baptism meant more than the infant baptism administered in the Catholic Church, because at least they were conscious of the one they had received under Menno or his father or him, which had been administered to them on confession of their faith in Jesus Christ, God's only Son and our Savior. "The infant baptism of the Catholics," he said, "is just so much water on top of an already wet baby." This brought a few chuckles from among the congregation.

A fellowship meal had been brought by the women, to which they then all assembled. Hearty encouragement was passed on from one to another, as the meal progressed. Some, to be sure, had not been able to bring very much at all, as they had not all been able to find work to provide for their families, so there were some desperately needy people to care for. Generally, Jacob and the church leaders sought to find out where the needs were greatest, so that they could assist in the best way possible. Families tended to be quite large, so the needs were often multiplied quite drastically, especially where someone who was poor before they fled simply didn't have enough to eat or clothes to wear. Families with similar-aged children were often asked if they could spare a piece of clothing for one or another child in the community. Overall, the fellowship time fulfilled its purpose admirably, with everyone having at least basic needs met.

The men of the community got together in one area for a discussion on what could be done for the community, now that they had heard there was no going back to Wuestenfelde. Various reports and rumors were heard about the activities of the armies of Tilly and Wallenstein, which continued their rampage of the province of Holstein. They seemed intent on destroying everything that belonged to Christian IV, who had dared to raise an army against them. Since most were mercenaries from other countries not involved in the war, they were not paid. Therefore, they relied on pillaging the countryside for their sustenance. Villages were easier to pillage than cities, so they tended to be the first targets. Hamburg, which was the largest city in northern Germany and a city of the Hanseatic League, was being spared, due to its strategic location for trade abroad and for supplying of the troops. Altona, living in its shadow, had become a refuge for Mennonites and Jews, who were especially targeted by the Catholic armies.

"We must invent some kind of business that will sustain us," one of the men lamented.

"We can't farm anymore," chimed in another, with the same strain in his voice.

"Some Wuestenfelders got involved with the Reformed people in the cloth industry in Bad Oldesloe. Would that be a possibility for us now? We could become spinners and weavers, and then sell the cloth to the merchants in Hamburg," Gerrit Roosen Sr. suggested.

"What about whaling?" another asked. "Some of our forefathers in the Netherlands were involved in the whaling industry, and the blubber sells well for lamp oil. I've even heard that the ribs are used by fashionable ladies as stays for their corsets."

"We can't take part in such worldliness – stays in corsets – what is the world coming to?" another remonstrated self-righteously.

"We don't have to make corset stays; we can just make lamp oil. Even Jesus used lamp oil as an example one time, so that would be OK," added someone else.

"Where would we get the boats, and who would teach us the trade?" ventured one of the more timid ones.

"We're land people, we don't work in boats," stated another, with finality.

"Have we tried to get work in Hamburg? Most of us have experience in a trade of some sort. Surely there is work there," replied another.

"Not with a war going on," someone cut in from the back. "Only essential jobs are continuing. Even the Lutherans can't find work."

"What about hiring ourselves out to help towns clean up after the army has been through their area?"

"No one has any money left to pay us, so we'd be wasting our time. The only pay we could hope for would be to pillage what has already been pillaged."

"It's springtime, so why not simply plant huge gardens in empty plots in the town, so that at least we get some kind of crop for next winter," suggested Jacob's cousin, who had grown up in Altona. He had not been active during the meeting, having kept quiet during the lively discussion. Jacob had invited him as a possible source of ideas that would fit into the situation they found themselves in. The Mennonites who had come to Altona earlier had adapted to city life over the years, and large community gardens were a thing of the past. But, this man remembered that there had been such large gardens in the past, usually on the edge of the village, and everyone took his turn in caring for parts of them.

That idea appealed to everyone. It represented something they had come from, it was practical, and it would provide for their needs in the future. Immediate needs would have to be considered on an *ad hoc* basis. With that, the meeting ended and the men joined their womenfolk for their return to whatever quarters they had been able to find.

"By the way, I heard from the Elder the other day, that our brethren, the Hutterites, have been driven out of Moravia by the Cardinal, and have fled to Slovakia. Some have also gone to Transylvania for refuge. It seems that the Catholics don't like us Anabaptists very much, no matter where we have fled. That is interesting, because we are actually using some of the wagons and carriages made by those Hutterites in Moravia," one of the leaders stated as an afterthought.

Jacob, as one of the leaders, took on himself a search for empty lots and fields near Altona, where the group might be able to plant gardens. He arranged for teams of horses and plows and harrows, to break up the unused soil. Manpower was in abundance, for many of the men had no work, so much of the finishing work on the fields was left to be done by hand. He had also been able to find potato seedlings and a variety of vegetable seed. Finally, they were ready for the planting. A great crowd of men, women and children, as well as young people, met together, and the seeds were distributed to the various groups assigned to the prepared plots. Off they went, most families making a meager picnic out of the event. Even the Dycks, with Suzie's lovely curls covered with a dark shawl, were there with the rest. She worked as much as she could on her own, avoiding contact with everyone as much as possible. One by one, members of their group conveyed their condolences to the girl, who expressed abject revulsion at any mention of her experience. Young people tried to get her attention and include her in their lighthearted banter, but she refused any contact with them. She was grieving, and the others around her could not penetrate the layers of grief and shame that surrounded her.

The difficulty of finding sufficient food for the group hung over the leaders. Men who were accustomed to working hard for their daily bread were destitute, demoralized and depressed. It was becoming more difficult all the time to get them roused up enough to go out and seek work. A few found work on neighboring farms, where they quickly fell into the patterns of spring work. The town hired some to help with work on the streets and bridges. Someone cared for the flowers that grew everywhere in prepared beds throughout the town square and in boxes hanging from the bridges, watering and weeding them regularly. Bit by bit every family was at least cared for at subsistence level. Everything that came in was shared among the lot, but still everyone had too little.

Health care was the next concern: Where and how could they find doctors to care for those who were injured, or women who were pregnant? With Rebekah in that condition, Jacob was especially concerned that proper medical care be made available, especially to expectant mothers and old people. There was some comfort in knowing that several of the women had experience as midwives, including Gerritt Roosen's wife, Martina, but there was no one to treat severe injuries or acute sicknesses. There was a doctor in Altona, but he was so overwhelmed with patients that the extra group of settlers could not depend on him, except in dire emergencies. There was no hospital, but the nuns in a convent at the edge of town were known to take in people for nursing care.

Not the least of the problems came with governmental restrictions placed upon this sect. It was not so bad in Altona, but in Hamburg, the city fathers – for the most part a group of prosperous Lutheran businessmen – were concerned about the image that their city would have among those with whom they traded. The Hanseatic cities circled the Baltic Sea, providing a solid trading block. Most of these cities had become Lutheran in the Reformation, so the Catholic armies were choosing one or another city to attack. Hamburgers wanted no part in the war, it could only damage their business; but they, in turn, picked on those who were different from them in their beliefs. The Mennonites and the Jews handily provided those targets.

Jacob and the other leaders were more than once working side-by-side with Jewish refugees, who had also come to the city and its neighboring town for safety. These were Sephardic Jews from Spain and Portugal, where the Inquisition was forcing out Muslims and Jews. They had come north, seeking refuge from political and religious persecution, just as the Mennonites were. Forbidden to farm, they seemed to drift into the heart of Hamburg, where they were soon engaged in money-lending and other financial pursuits, using what small cash reserves they had been able to hoard and bring with them to gain more. The attitude of northern Europe toward the Jews during the Middle Ages had been very negative, for it was believed that they were the ones who had crucified God's Son, who was the Saviour of the Europeans; they were therefore hated and feared by Christians everywhere. In addition, unfounded but readily accepted rumours circulated that they were suspected of making child sacrifices. As a result, the Jews also looked for a building in Altona, where the restrictions on worship were less severe. Finding none, they approached the Mennonites, who had found an empty machine shed for their worship services, and asked whether they could use the shed on Saturdays, when the Mennonites were not using it. That proved convenient for all, so an agreement was made between the two woebegone groups.

With great effort on the part of the leaders, and a spirit of cooperation on the part of all the families, a semblance of order and routine set into the community. The community, in turn, set about healing the internal situations that insisted on raising their heads from time to time. The Dycks were especially singled out for loving attention, but they were withdrawing more and more into a legalistic, anger-driven world view that did not seem to reflect the views of Menno, and they were withdrawing more and more unto themselves. Jonathan remained on the council, but he seldom contributed to the discussion. Jacob and the others prayed earnestly for him and his family, especially for Suzie, that healing would come.

Chapter 3

"Everything is gone!" exclaimed Rebekah, as she and the other women went to one of the garden plots to harvest peas and beans. To be sure, not only was there no fruit on the plants, but the plants themselves had been torn up and scattered. Returning to their homes, they met women returning from the other plots, and every one of them had been destroyed.

"Who could have done that?" they all chorused.

"I don't think it was anyone living in Altona; the people here have taken us in willingly enough."

"What about the Jews? They always do sneaky things to their enemies." someone else chimed in.

"I doubt that they would do something like that to us, when we allowed them to use our shed for their synagogue," reflected Rebekah, in return.

"What about that man who bought your horses and wagon? He looked like a sneak to me," another woman observed.

"He paid in good gold, so we couldn't very well complain about his looks," rejoined Rebekah, a bit peeved that the blame was being laid close to her door.

"But he was an agent of the Catholic army, and he was probably spying on our situation, to see what they could do to us without attacking us with the whole army. That would have aroused outright retaliation, but this kind of thing accomplishes just as much without anyone being able to fight back," the other woman reasoned.

"That is definitely a possibility. I'll talk with Jacob about it," Rebekah replied, realizing that this was being laid squarely on her doorstep.

That evening she mentioned the day's disappointments to Jacob, along with the suggested culprits who might have done this to them. Jacob pondered for a long time before replying. His lips were pursed, and he bit his lower lip so hard that it blanched. Alternately, he worked his tongue around behind his lips, causing his face to distort into strange shapes.

"We cannot use the sword to fight the sword," he finally got something out. "The Bible says that, if your enemy hungers, feed him. I guess the soldiers were hungry, so they took our vegetables for themselves. They were definitely our enemies, for they even pulled up the plants, so that no more would grow. I guess that's just a continuation of what they have done everywhere they went, including our beloved Wuestenfelde."

"What are we going to eat, now that our only source of food is gone?" asked Rebekah plaintively.

Jacob shrugged his shoulders, "We men were talking today about a possible industry we could begin. We know about wagon-making, so why not start a factory where we make good solid wagons? We could also make carriages for the city folk. This would provide work for many men, and it would provide money for our sustenance through the winter." Jacob seemed to have a very clear idea of how to go about starting this business. The idea seemed good to Rebekah, and she did not ask what she really wanted to ask, which was, "What are we and the other families going to eat this evening and tomorrow, now that our summer gardens are gone?" Instead, she shrugged her shoulders and went back to her kitchen to see if she could find anything with which to feed her family that evening.

Whom You Will Serve

Now that the army had taken to stealing their garden produce, there seemed to be little hope for the future among the Mennonites. Jacob and the other leaders worked day-in-day-out to seek ways to alleviate the desperate needs of the refugees. He was looking more gaunt each day, as sleep and food deprivation took their toll. His whining children added to the misery each evening, as he came home in an even more hopeless state.

Getting the wagon factory going proved to be a greater effort than anyone had reckoned. Finding the tools to accomplish the work, and a place to do the work, as well as raw materials for the construction took one or another of the men's full-time attention. The leaders finally decided that it would be best to use the shed they were meeting in for church, and which the Jews were using on Saturdays for their worship, as the location of the wagon factory, too. It would mean putting all their tools and pieces of wagon away each weekend, so that worship benches could be put out, but at least it was a relatively large and open building. Among themselves they found enough tools to begin work, and enough skilled craftsmen to be able to fashion wagons capable of handling tough jobs for a long time.

It was during the preparation phase, while they were installing the chain hoist to the ceiling beam that it happened. Gerritt Roosen, one of the leading men of the Mennonite community, was struck by a falling piece of equipment, and killed instantly. The men stood around in horror at the scene, but there was nothing they could do, except to carry his body out for the women to prepare for burial. Martina was notified, and Rebekah went with her children to comfort the new widow. The men knew instinctively that they must continue to work at getting the place ready to begin work. Reluctantly, but with great resolve, they made themselves get the job done.

A week later, the first wagon was ready for sale, and the man responsible to find contacts for purchase was able to sell it for a reasonable price. With that money, they could buy more wood and iron to make another wagon, and they had a bit extra to buy some cheap barley with which to make coarse bread or cooked cereal or soup.

Those who worked on farms, or who had been able to rent farms of their own, were able to supply a few things for the group, but the armies were also targeting these sources. It seemed to the group as though someone was informing the armies of the various locations. Suspicion began to creep into the group, and one or another was singled out for special attention. Soon the leaders had to investigate these allegations. It was both a social and a clerical problem, so Jacob and the deacons were called into the discussion together with the Schultze and Community Council.

"How are we going to find out who is responsible for informing the army of our food sources?" Isaac Klassen asked to begin the meeting.

"Just going to the accused people and asking them won't give us anything," Paul Wiebe responded, glumly. "They'll just lie and accuse us of being snoopers."

"Still, we must do something. If we don't, the others won't believe we are doing our job as leaders and as deacons," Jacob added. "Does someone have a good idea of how we might find the one or ones who are informing our enemies?"

"Perhaps we can take turns standing guard somewhere, to see who is going where no one else goes," proposed Anton Kroeker.

"The kind of person that would betray us would find out who was standing guard and where we are, and simply avoid us," scowled Isaac Funk. "We have to figure out how the person is making the contact, and do some police work in that area."

"Isaac, you are pretty good at that kind of activity, I think, why don't you begin to do some sleuthing?" Jacob agreed. "Maybe you could get Anton to work with you, and see if you can come up with something we can all hear. Then we can determine how we are going to deal with such a person."

"We'll have to ban him from the church and from his family, for sure," said Cornelius Janzen. "Our church treats traitors very severely."

"Perhaps," said Jacob, authoritatively, "but we also deal with each other in Christian love."

"We'll not kill him outright, then," replied Cornelius curtly, "that will be Christian love enough, I would think."

"Now, now, Cornelius, let's wait to find out who it is and what his circumstances are, before we jump to conclusions about what to do with him," Jacob and the deacons chorused.

The meeting ended at that. Isaac and Anton conversed for a bit, strategizing their approach. Anton knew that the soldiers were often found at a Gasthaus near the boundary between Hamburg and Altona. He would go there that evening, dressed as much as possible like a resident of the city, and trying to disguise himself as much as possible, to avoid detection. Isaac would talk to a few of those who were most vociferous about their suspicions and see if they had any ideas who it might be.

Jacob had all he could do to work at his carpentry shop, supervising the wagon factory, and preparing messages for the Sunday services. He could not spare any more energy for the sleuthing, so he was forced to rely on his two faithful men. Although he did not get much work in his carpentry shop, he was able to keep food on the table most of the time, and did not have to rely on the distribution going on among the group, from that which could be found on the farms and that which could be bought with profits from the wagon factory, or through donations from the townsfolk of Altona.

The group that had suggested whaling did not give up on their idea. There was money to be made in whale oil. Most of the lamps in the city burned that fuel. To be sure, they were not interested in the rib bones as corset stays, but even those could be sold for a profit, perhaps closing their eyes to what they might be used for by others. They investigated their options, and came up with a boat for hire, with the owner willing to train them in the art of whaling, and in the skill of sailing a ship in a blustery North Sea. It would mean being away from their families for lengthy times, but when they would return, there would be profit for everyone in the business. The leaders agreed to allow them to venture out in this dangerous work. Since the battle was not at sea at that time, they felt secure that they would be relatively unmolested in their work. Soon there were five men leaving for the port to begin their new adventure. Three of them had families, and two were young singles, trying to get started in something that would support a wife and children later.

Women, at the suggestion of Martina Roosen, took out their spinning wheels and their spindles, and began making thread for the weavers, who also took out small family looms that they had brought along, to weave the thread into cloth that could be sold in the market, or through agents in the Hanseatic League. Bit by bit the families were able to establish small household businesses that would help sustain the group. Martina Roosen felt, though, that it would be wonderful, if they were able to manufacture hosiery, as well, but that would have to wait for now.

All profits were shared among them, so that no one went without at the expense of another. Jacob occasionally had to remind someone or other of that policy, as the temptation to withhold part of the profits for their own use was pretty strong. He reminded them of Ananias and Sapphira, of the terrible price that they had to pay for doing the same thing. Above all things, the patterns of life outlined in the Bible, particularly in the early church and in the gospels, were set as examples for the group to follow. The Mennonites did not ever hold all things in common and live communally, as their Anabaptist brothers, the Hutterites did, but they believed that, in such times of stress and danger, the communal sharing of all goods and profits was essential for the good of the entire group. It was the job of the pastor and of the deacons, as well as community leaders, to enforce this policy.

A week went by without any further incident of vandalism or thievery. Isaac and Anton had nothing special to report, though they had diligently done their duty to find out what they could. As so often happens in a case such as this, when the community is close-knit and largely related to one another, a loose word on the part of someone gossiping by the village well provided the clue that helped them to find the culprits. It was not long before they had evidence for themselves, as they followed up on the lead brought to them by Isaac's wife, who had heard the idle word from another woman, whose husband was apparently involved. As it turned out, the woman herself, Freda Guenther, was involved together with her husband, Wilhelm Guenther; another man, Gustav Wall, was involved, as well. Soon the three were locked in various rooms in one of the community houses. Rebekah took the five Guenther children in, to look after them, while the parents were incarcerated.

A council of the deacons and the community leaders was called. Jacob chaired the meeting. He opened by saying, "Men, we have met to decide what to do for the good of our Mennonite community. Wilhelm and Freda Guenther and Gustav Wall are alleged to have betrayed us to the Catholic army, which is seeking to destroy us. According to our sources, they have revealed to them where our food stores are, and where our gardens were located, as well as some of our other activities, that would provide the army information on which to act against us. Isaac Funk and Anton Kroeker have acted on our behalf to try to find out who was doing this, and they have brought Wilhelm and Freda Guenther and Gustav Wall to us, to decide whether or not there is enough proof of their guilt to act against them. Isaac, could you please tell us what you found out."

A hush fell over the group of leading men as Isaac Funk made his way to the front. He cleared his throat and began hesitantly, "Men and brothers, Anton and I were lying in wait for over a week in places where we were likely to spot someone dealing with the soldiers, but we found nothing. It was a chance remark by Freda Guenther that gave them away, and it was my wife, Julia, that told me about what she had heard. Apparently the Guenthers and Gustav felt that, if we had not been so pacifistic, we would not have been in this situation. They were taking revenge on us for, in their words, running away from the situation, instead of taking a stand against the Catholic army. Now, I suggest that the Guenthers be brought in one at a time and then Mr. Wall, and we interrogate them individually." At that, Jacob nodded to Isaac, and he and Anton went to fetch the prisoners. In the meantime, the men discussed possible questions to ask each of the accused. Soon the sound of approaching scuffles was heard, and in came Isaac and Anton, with Wilhelm Guenther between them, his hands bound behind him, and with rope shackles on his ankles, to prevent his running away. He was thrust to the front of the group.

"Wilhelm Guenther, we would like to know what you did to betray our group to the army," began Jacob.

"It's none of your business!" snapped the cornered man, showing his antagonistic spirit.

"We have gathered all the evidence we need, Wilhelm, you may as well own up to what you have done. Your wife has already confessed," continued Jacob.

"You can leave my wife out of this," he snapped again.

"Wilhelm, did you contact the army to provide information to them about our stores and our activities, that allowed them to single us out for vandalism and thievery?" Jacob asked firmly. Silence prevailed.

"Wilhelm, your silence will not save you," said George Toews, the Schultze, or leader of the community. "As Jacob has said, there is enough evidence to prove you guilty."

"Then hang me, if you wish," snapped the accused man again, "you won't get anything out of me. Your pacifism has damned you to live like animals without a burrow, and with nothing to eat and nothing to wear, except castoffs from everyone else. I can't live like that, so you can do away with me now."

"Take him back to where you are keeping him, and bring his wife," ordered Jacob to his two men. Soon they returned with Freda Guenther between them, hands bound but without shackles. She was weeping, and her step faltered.

"Freda Guenther, you and your husband have been accused of betraying us to the Catholic soldiers, who have used that information to destroy our means of livelihood. Do you confess to this?" Jacob tried to be as tender as possible, but to get to the point immediately.

A loud wail came from the stricken woman, but no words. Finally, she managed to gasp between sobs, "Where are my children? I want my children."

"They are being well looked after, and they will be well looked after, regardless of what happens to you, so please tell us the truth about what you have done," stated George Toews.

"You and your stupid ideas about not taking the sword . . . that's insulting to us. We should have defended ourselves against the army – there probably weren't as many in the detachment that destroyed Wuestenfelde as there were of us. We could have offered at least an honorable resistance," she bellowed.

"Did you, or did you not, inform the soldiers of our stores and our activities? Yes, or no?" The Schultze was raising his voice by this time. The pastor looked at him, as if to ask him to keep the questioning low-key, please.

"I'm not saying anything. I obviously already said too much," sneered Freda.

"Take her away and get Gustav Wall," commanded Jacob. The men took the struggling woman back to her cell and went for the third person. As he entered, similarly shackled and tied up as Wilhelm had been, the Schultze took over the questioning.

"Gustav, we have evidence that you were involved with the Guenthers in betraying us to the Catholic army. Is that true?" he began.

"You can all be damned," Gustav shouted. "I don't care what you think. I am an individual, and I have a right to my own mind. I don't have to follow your ideas of how I should live. I can make my own decisions. I don't need you."

"That may be true, Gustav, but we are here as a group because we all believe one thing," began Jacob, "and we fled, because of that belief. We think that this is what the Bible teaches us to do, when the enemy wants to destroy us. The early Christians fled persecution – just read the book of Acts, and you'll see that time and time again, the Christians had to leave one place and go to another, because they were persecuted."

"Don't preach to me," he spat. "I'll do what I like, when I like, and how I like. You don't have any authority over me."

"You admit, then, that you went to the soldiers with information about us, which they then used to attack our means of survival as a group," George suggested.

"I won't admit anything," snarled Gustav.

"Take him away," ordered Jacob again to his two helpers. They took him away, snarling and spitting all the way back to his room.

The men fell strangely silent. What were they going to do, in that none of the accused had admitted guilt? To be sure, the evidence they had, though somewhat circumstantial, was quite conclusive.

Jacob took the lead. "This seems to be a direct attack on the beliefs that have guided us since the days of Menno," he began. "Our unwillingness to take the sword is what sets us apart from other Protestants, and we believe it is taught us from the Bible, not to bear the sword. These people have attacked one of our fundamental doctrines, so as a church, we must act."

George began on behalf of the community leaders, "They undermined the security of our whole community, which is a terrible crime. Everyone is suffering more, because they did what they did to all of us. We must act on behalf of the community. Perhaps we could get the cooperation of the town constables, to pass sentence upon them. Surely all of Altona will feel the effects of their crime."

"In that their crime is both against the community and against the church, we will have to act separately, when it comes to dealing with their actions," Jacob ventured. "May I have the deacons come with me for a meeting about this, please." He began moving to another place, where they could meet separately from the community leaders, who were huddling around George Toews, to discuss community action against these traitors.

"Each of them expressed the thought that they really do not want to belong to our church any more. They disagree on one of our fundamental teachings, so they really don't stand with us as a body anymore," began Jacob.

"We should put them under the ban and not allow Wilhelm and Freda to be together any more, and not allow any of them to take communion or to vote in any church business," stated one of the deacons firmly.

"If they are not really members in their hearts, the ban won't do any good. They'll just go somewhere else and continue what they have been thinking all along," reasoned Jacob. "I think we should simply excommunicate them out of the church. Then we don't have anything more to do with them. If they continue to betray us, we would simply have to accept the fact that we do not retaliate. We flee again."

"That means we are taking the punishment for their crime," added another, puzzled.

"How do you mean that?" asked Jacob, with a questioning look on his face.

"Well, if they go free, and we have to live with them anyway, in spite of what they have done, we are the ones who are suffering the punishment, not they, for their sins."

"Isn't that the way it was with Christ?" asked Jacob in return. "He didn't sin, but He took our sins upon Him, so that we could be set free. Besides, we can always hope that they repent and seek to come back into the church." That thought was not immediately popular, but, biting their lips in frustration, the men slowly nodded their assent.

In the other group, the discussion was similar. The conclusion was similar, as well. It was not practical to keep them locked up. Mennonites were not known for having jails. Nor could they, as a refugee community within the larger community of Altona and Holstein, demand that the culprits leave town and never bother them again, unless the civil authorities of Altona and of Holstein would agree to take over their policing. George would check into that, but in the meantime, they must let them go free with a warning and whatever punishment the church might levy against them.

The two groups met and discussed what they had concluded, which seemed to everyone to be the right thing to do. Isaac and Anton were commissioned to bring the three accused before them again, this time taking half a dozen men with them to enforce their cooperation.

George took the lead this time. "Because you have acted against the whole community of Mennonites here in Altona, we as elected leaders must discipline you. But, because we cannot act without the consent of the Duke of Holstein, we are limited in what we can do. Here is what we have decided: We will go to the civil authorities in Altona and Holstein, to see if they will take on the case. In the meantime, you will be set free to go back to your homes. You will from henceforth, however, cease to be considered as part of our Mennonite community, and you will therefore not receive any more benefits from our group efforts, nor will you be allowed to work in our projects. Any privileges granted by the Duke to our group will no longer apply to you." He nodded to Jacob to state his part in the decision.

"Because you have attacked one of the fundamental teachings of the church you belong to, we must deal with that, as well. You have clearly stated that you do not agree with our pacifism, and that we are doing wrong in acting on our belief in this principle," began Jacob, with clarity, but with a slight quiver in his voice. "It grieves me to tell you this, but the deacons and I have agreed that you must all be excommunicated from the Mennonite church, and that you will no longer be able to take communion with us. Since we could not enforce the ban anyway, we will not impose it upon you, in relation to one another as husband and wife, but you will be shunned by everyone in the church from now on. Your case will be brought before the church next time we meet, and everyone in the church membership will be informed to have nothing more to do with you, either privately or publically. Untie them and let them go, please."

The three hurriedly shuffled out of the room, as Jacob called after them, "Your children will be brought to your house right away." He assigned Isaac and Anton to this final task, which they took on with dignity.

Chapter 4

Problems caused by something as grave as treason in the group do not easily go away, and this was no exception. The Guenthers and Gustav insisted on coming to church anyway, so it became necessary for the strong men of the church to forcibly remove them Sunday after Sunday. This caused so much commotion that tender people within the group began insisting that they should leave them alone – Jesus tolerated Judas among His disciples, until that disciple had done his nasty work in their midst. The leaders, including Jacob, did not agree. They felt that, in the tradition of the Flemish Mennonites, which their Friesian group had adopted as their own, they must hold a strong line on misbehaving members, and use excommunication and the ban when necessary. The group soon became divided, some taking one side and some taking the other. Leaders were found among the dissenting group, and soon they had decided to meet separately from the main group. They were, after all, more spiritually in tune than the other group, which was obviously not following the one and only, true biblical teaching. Naturally, the Guenthers and Gustav Wall gravitated to that group, where they were coddled as much as was possible, to demonstrate what they thought was true Christian love to their wayward brethren and sister.

"What are we going to do with our dissenting group?" asked Rebekah at supper.

"I'd rather not discuss it in front of the children," replied Jacob.

"They know. They see it every day and especially every Sunday," rationalized Rebekah.

"There is nothing we can do," whispered Jacob. "Unless we go against everything we believe about what the Bible teaches us, we have to let people choose their own way of living. All we can do is teach what we believe the Bible to say to us, and I believe we are doing that. When people do something that is wrong against us, Jesus told us not to retaliate. God said, 'Vengeance is mine, I will repay.' We are not to retaliate when others do something against us – and that goes for you, too, children." Jacob had noticed some jostling behind the table, and he was quick to remonstrate against that. There was immediate compliance, for the children had more than once experienced his strong disciplinary actions against them, should they continue when he had told them to stop. The incongruity of what he was doing with what he was saying was not apparent to him at all. A father's position before his children was that of God before the church, his duty before God was to punish disobedience in his children. The only restriction on that was, as far as Jacob could think, that it should be done in love, and with their good in mind, not brutally or in a rage.

"But we'll be a laughingstock to the others in Altona," continued Rebekah. "If we all claim to have the truth, but we can't agree with one another, what kind of testimony is that to the townsfolk?"

"We can't do anything about what people in town will think. They will think what they want, anyway. Each one comes at his thoughts from his own perspective on life. The Catholics believe that anyone who believes differently from what the Church teaches is wrong. They can live as they please, but as long as they uphold the sacraments required by their Church, they will somehow be saved. The Lutherans believe that, once you are baptized as a baby, you are part of the family of God, and as long as you attend church faithfully and give your tithe to the church, you can live pretty much as you please after that, and you will be saved in the end. The Calvinists believe that God ordains some to salvation and some to damnation, and once you find out that you are predestined to salvation, you will follow God's way instinctively. Just to be sure, they set a lot of rules, just like we do, to guide the flock in the truth of God's Word."

"How can we testify to the truth, when everyone has his or her own truth?" Rebekah was not letting up on Jacob. These things were bothering her greatly. Just having had the Guenther children in her home for a few hours had opened up a flood of questions about these basic issues of church life. She was totally unaware that her question formed the basis of the philosophy of Postmodernism, which wouldn't come into vogue until three hundred years later.

"It is not our work to convert people; the Holy Spirit must do that. We must simply live out our faith before the world, and He will do the rest," assured Jacob. "It has been like that since the beginning of the Church of Christ, and it will be to the day that Christ comes to take it to Himself."

Rebekah, always the practical one, was not so convinced that this was the way it should be handled. She felt that people should be compelled to come into the feast, as the Lord had said in one of His parables. Those who made excuses would be punished eternally, as would those who tried to enter the feast without the proper wedding garment. There were obvious rules in church life, and they needed to be enforced. That was her rule of faith. Just how people were to be compelled to enter the feast was a mystery to her, but she believed that God would sort out the mystery. This discussion did not end in agreement; it was more nearly an uneasy truce.

For Jacob, the first occurrence of something to do with the shunning was when Wilhelm showed up for work at the wagon plant. He kindly told the man that he was no longer part of this group, and that he was not welcome to participate in the work anymore. Wilhelm insisted on continuing, and several of the others were called to escort him out of the premises. He returned the following day, and the following, and each time Jacob and the men had to forcibly remove him. That took valuable time from the production, so the men had to work extra hard to catch up. A son of one of the men, who was old enough to learn a trade, was brought into the group to carry Wilhelm's share of the work. Wilhelm was left to find work elsewhere, which he finally did in the shop in Hamburg where Jacob had been working previously in cabinetry, until the wagon shop took all of his time. Gustav was not heard from for some time, until someone reported that he had seen him walking drunkenly on the streets of Hamburg, a haggard wreck of a man, hardly recognizable.

One day not long after, word came to Jacob and the leaders, that the Plague had hit the other church group, and that Wilhelm and Freda were both lying at death's door. Once again, Rebekah took their children in with hers. Anxiously the entire community kept watch, to see in which house the pestilence would strike next. Eventually it was reported that Gustav had succumbed to it, and had been found dead on the street and carried away for quick burial by city workers. Jacob and the leaders began wondering why it should have been the very people who had betrayed them, who were struck down first.

"God is judging them for their betrayal," said George Toews. "We were right in banning them from our fellowship."

"Maybe there is another reason," suggested Jacob, "they were in contact with the soldiers who destroyed our crops. Perhaps the soldiers brought the Plague into our midst."

"I did hear from one of the traders that the company of soldiers garrisoned near to us here has come down with it, so that is possible," responded the Schultze.

"That would also answer the other question that has been running through my mind since the gardens and crops were destroyed, and that is: Why haven't they come back to do more damage?" Jacob added. "If they got sick and died, that would explain why they didn't come back."

"That certainly seems to be the best explanation then," concluded George.

"At first I thought maybe our people had gotten it from the rats that persist in coming back, but perhaps the soldiers got it from them originally in their camp," Jacob was musing in areas where his understanding had not yet gone.

Rebekah kept watch on the Guenther children, but none seemed to be coming down with any of the plague's symptoms. She also watched her own family, in case they picked it up, but for the moment, no signs were present. Within a couple of days, however, word came to the Derksens that both Wilhelm and Freda had succumbed to the effects of the plague. The breakaway group had not ordained any minister yet, so Jacob was called on to lead the burial service for them, even though they had been excommunicated from the church. Reluctantly he accepted the invitation, realizing that there would be many a mouth set into motion over his decision. Since there were no relatives of the Guenthers in the group, Rebekah simply insisted on keeping the five children as her own. This extra work, in addition to her own pregnancy, was going to take its toll on her strength, but she was convinced it was the right thing for her to do. Jacob, on the other hand, was not nearly as convinced, as he would need to earn more, in order to feed and clothe the extra bodies. Still, he saw the logic in his wife's decision and did not speak against her, though he wondered how a family that had more than doubled so quickly could be united into one.

"Will we let them keep their last name?" inquired Rebekah, late at night, when all had been put to bed.

"Yes, I think it would not be good to blot the family name out," replied Jacob, thoughtfully.

"That will always be confusing for our own children," his wife rejoined.

"It will be anyway, no matter how we handle it. Once they are old enough to understand that their parents died of the Plague, and we took them in, they will accept the fact that their names are different from ours. We don't have to mention the problems that led to their catching the disease unless they ask about it."

"I guess we'll start a school in fall, like we had in Wuestenfelde, won't we?" Rebekah surmised.

"No one has mentioned that in any of our meetings. There have been so many things to do and so many decisions of an immediate nature, that we have not thought that far ahead," replied Jacob, surprised at the new thought. "I'll have to bring it up at our next meeting, because we certainly will need that." As an afterthought, he added, "Especially now that we have so many children in the house, it will be good if at least some of them can be in school during the day. That will help you get a bit more rest before the baby comes."

They chuckled together over this, and prepared for bed

Chapter 5

Jacob was at the wagon factory the next day when an official from the town of Altona stopped by. Curious as to what brought him to them Jacob cautiously began to speak with him. Another reason why Jacob spoke with him, and not the others, was that Jacob had learned High German, and the others spoke Dutch and Low German only. As he greeted the man, he noticed him observing the others at their various tasks. Some of their work for the assembly of the wagons was quite clumsy, as they had only primitive tools. What was lacking in technology, however, was made up in manpower and willingness. The town official was both amazed and amused at their camaraderie and good will.

"I have come to ask a favor of you," the man began. "The Plague has taken everyone from our town's blacksmith shop, so that no one can shoe horses or fashion iron into things of use. If you could find someone with blacksmithing skills, who could run it, we would be very happy."

"We have a small forge here, to fashion the things we need for wagons, but it is far too small for some of the work. We also have some ideas for the manufacture of farm implements that we are unable to put into practice, because our tools are inadequate," replied Jacob.

"Our forge is quite large, and the shop itself is very roomy and built of brick, so there is very little danger of fire. You could easily move your whole operation into it and run your plant from there," the man said, getting quite convincing. He seemed desperate to find help for their need among the Mennonites.

"May I come along with you, so we can look at it together?" asked Jacob. The man seemed very relieved, and invited him to come immediately.

As they walked to the location of the blacksmith shop, they chatted about a number of things, including the effects of the Plague upon the town and upon Hamburg. Most importantly, they talked about its effects on the army that was camped nearby. Jacob learned that most of the soldiers had gotten sick, and many had died, so that the camp was now deserted. There would be no more raids for the foreseeable future. Both Jacob and the man were glad of that.

The shop proved to be all that the man had said. It had served both as a place where the farmers could have their horses and oxen shod, and where small metal fabrication jobs could be carried out. One specialty had been the turning of iron to make wrought iron fences and gates. Jacob knew that Isaac Funk and Anton Kroeker both had experience in running a blacksmith shop, so he began immediately to think how the whole operation of the wagon factory could be moved to the new quarters, and what possibilities there might be for expanding the work into the production of farm implements. As an additional item, they could continue to work in wrought iron for various practical applications. It never once entered his mind that wrought iron could be considered by other Mennonites as simply useless art; all products needed to be practical, as far as they were concerned.

He discussed the terms for leasing the business from the town, and returned to his own shop to see how the men were doing with their work. The decision to move the shop would have to be brought before the Schultze, George Toews, and their leadership council, so he did not mention anything of the discussions with the town official to his men.

That evening he returned home to find that Rebekah was in deep distress. Both Jake and Heidi had symptoms of the Plague, and their great age almost certainly sealed their doom, if that were the case. Jacob wanted to tell her of the great fortune that had befallen their group, but when he learned of his parents' illness, he bit his lip. Anxiously they waited through the night, bathing them to cool the scorching fever, but all to no avail. Shortly before morning, first Jake, and then soon after, Heidi, went to their eternal rest. Their wizened bodies seemed even more emaciated, after the fever had taken its toll. The broken blood vessels had left great dark blotches all over their bodies. As Jacob quietly closed his parents' eyes, he gave his wife a hug around the shoulders and left to begin arrangements for their funeral.

As he went about his work, he thought how strange it was, that God seemed to take delight in the incongruous – giving great blessings, as He took away dearly loved ones.

The funeral was one of the great events of the Mennonite group that had sought refuge in Altona. It seemed that everyone was present, and even the outcasts who had left the main group, now that the Plague had taken away so many of them, came to pay their respects to the man who had been their pastor for so many years, and whom they had come to respect, along with his energetic wife, who had been the center of every church picnic, and who had taught so many of them or their children. No one seemed to care that these people came, as all shared in the grief of losing a couple that all had come to love and cherish. Jacob preached a message of redemption and love, emphasizing God's love for sinners and His Spirit of new life, even though the earthly body was subject to sickness and death. The earthly man or woman was also subject to sin, and God's Spirit's work was to renew the inner person to walk in newness of life through faith. Arrangements had been made to bury them in the Mennonite cemetery that had been in use since early in the century, and that is where the caskets were now carried in solemn procession.

Once the funeral was over, Jacob asked George Toews to call a meeting of the community council. That evening, the men met. Jacob presented the proposal made by the official from Altona, emphasizing that they could expand their work to include many other things they could sell on the market, so as to provide for their families through the next winter, which would come in due course. The men listened intently, nodding here or there, or pursing their lips when questions came to mind. When he finished, George opened the floor for questions.

"Where will we sell the things we could make there?" inquired one of the men.

"I think we have built up a good reputation with the wagons we have been able to sell so far, and through those contacts, we should be able to sell farm implements or other things useful around the house," responded Jacob. "Besides, I think the quality of our wagons will increase, as we have better equipment with which to build them. Our wheel hubs and our metal tires will be able to be done much faster and better in a larger forge. We'll also have more room to work, so we can be making several wagons at once. That will increase our efficiency, and of course, our profits."

"What is all this going to cost us?" another man queried. "Remember, we don't have a lot of money to invest in anything."

"The town official said that we could begin using the equipment and the shop without any investment, just so that we are available to shoe horses and oxen, and to make repairs to equipment brought in by local people," Jacob said. "The service to the community is worth more to the town than any possible income from the lease. Once we are established – let's say next spring, we can begin to pay a reasonable lease on the shop, but by then we'll have the money we need. The town is trying to help us get established. They see in us valuable workers with skills they can use. They do not even think about our having a different faith from theirs. So many have come here recently because of the war, they no longer look at a person's religion, when they think of what will work out well for the town. It is growing so quickly now, that the town council is scrambling to find enough space for all the new things that are happening here." Jacob had learned a great deal from the town official that had been sent to speak with him. He was not aware that this was the mayor himself, speaking on behalf of his town council, the aspirations they had for their town, now that it seemed to be a magnet for refugees from many parts of Europe. Jew and Gentile alike seemed to find contentment in its confines.

Rebekah, meanwhile, was left with the clearing out of Jake and Heidi's things, in addition to looking after her own children and the added brood from the Guenthers. Her own pregnancy added to the drudgery, and there were times when she felt she must surely collapse from sheer exhaustion. Benjamin was just old enough to be a great help to her, holding the other end of something she was working with, or carrying things here or there for her. For shorter periods of time, Joshua and Mary could also be of help, and Elizabeth helped most by playing with the Guenther children: Susan – 8, Nickolas – 7, Jonathan – 6, Agnes – 4, and Willy – 3. Mary and Joshua also helped quite a bit in this assignment, when their mother didn't need them for specific jobs.

Mourning was not something the Mennonites carried out to any great length, or with any visible emotion. They cared greatly for their departed loved ones, but practicality ruled every part of the cycle of their lives, and death was part of that cycle. Jacob hid his feelings well, carrying on the day-to-day work in supervising the moving of the wagon shop to the blacksmith shop, introducing Isaac and Anton to their new forge and other equipment, and discussing with the men some of the plans he had for adding to their production. Rebekah loved her parents-in-law very much, but she also realized that they had experienced a very long and full life, and their time to meet their Maker had come. It was only a shame that they had to depart in such a miserable way. She, like many Mennonites, reduced her sorrow through the application of her energies to more and harder work. Work as a way of mourning – that seemed to be the way for all of them to heal from such great loss.

The community leaders met again to discuss what to do about the breakaway group. They had not been excommunicated from the church, but had left on their own volition. Therefore, it was decided to simply take them back into their fellowship, if they were willing to acknowledge the group as expressive of their beliefs. Jacob was asked to meet with the various couples, and to find out what their feelings and beliefs were.

Having thus met with each of the families, Jacob could assure the leadership that the families were genuinely people of faith in Christ alone, and that they felt deeply remorseful for their strong reaction previously. It was agreed that they would be quietly accepted back into fellowship, without any formalities, and all seemed to appreciate that. What would be the questions on the part of the original group was left to be answered when the problem arose. For the moment, the effect the Plague had again had on their congregation was enough to sober all of them, and to retard any thoughts of separation from the group.

Wagon production increased dramatically, once the group was more familiar with the new equipment they now had at their disposal. The quality of workmanship also increased, making the wagons easier to sell. Profits increased, allowing Jacob to hire more men, and to lay aside something for the other projects he had in mind. George and the community leaders reminded him often that some of the profits needed to go into the community trust fund, to be used in case of emergencies and to care for widows and old people in the congregation. This Jacob was careful to do right from the start of his enterprise, as he cared deeply for his flock, both young and old, both productive members and those who could no longer contribute to the general welfare of the group. Martina Roosen was one of those recently widowed through the accident to her husband while working in the factory, so he was doubly concerned that she and others in her state were well looked after.

The blacksmiths reveled in the new equipment available to them, and they began making simple items for household use – cooking pots, dustpans, fireplace implements, lampstands and wall brackets – as well as horseshoes and harness parts. Forged chains also sold well. The ornamental wrought iron work became practically-oriented, as the men applied their faith to their jobs. When specially ordered by their larger community, however, they demonstrated an amazing ability to make ornamental banisters and gates, as well.

Soon Jacob discussed plans for farm implements with Isaac and Anton, who would be required to use the forge to bend and fashion larger pieces of iron than they had ever worked with before. Together, they thought of ways to make it possible, so that the planned farm equipment could be constructed. They also discussed the crew that would be needed, for the forge would be heated with the aid of the huge bellows that none of them had ever operated before. This would require some strong young men, who could work in a very warm environment. Still, the possibilities of increasing production in the plant outweighed any other problems that they could imagine beforehand. A few items would have to be ordered, and Jacob thought he had a contact for those things. He made a note of them, to bring up at the meeting of the leaders.

Rebekah was managing fairly well with the Guenther children, but three-year-old Willy was being quite stubborn about potty training. This took much of her time and energy for the next while. The other problem was that the Guenther children needed clothing, for they had not had very much to bring with them. Hand-me-downs could only be trusted for so much; some things were better gotten new. She had no time to sew things, and very little with which to sew anyway. The other ladies heard about her plight, and they dug deeply into their children's unused clothing, and they found enough to help out in the immediate need. The community needed to work together, to help one another, and this was one of those times, when that help was much appreciated.

A second planting of some not-too-delicate vegetables was coming along nicely, so there was hope of something to relieve the monotony of porridge morning, noon and night. Beans, of the haricot variety that had been brought over from America very recently, had found their way into northern Germany, and they obtained some seeds, which they sowed in large fields. These looked especially hopeful, as they were already blooming. So far they had been able to get several different kinds of grain with their profits from the wagon factory, as well as some from the sale of their cloth, so the meals were becoming varied, with cooked oats for breakfast, barley for lunch, and rye for supper. A few bags of wheat flour were also gotten, along with some sourdough starter, so an occasional meal of fresh white bread was now possible. Milk was scarce, but it had been all along. It was good that Jacob had insisted on bringing their cow, or there would have been none for their children. The calf had long since been slaughtered for its meat, as they had nothing to feed it anyway. The Mennonite farmers who had been able to lease farms, as well as those who found work on neighboring farms, were able to glean a few things from their acreages, which they contributed into the community larder. The hardworking Mennonites had also become known to many long-established farmers, who contributed to their welfare, as well. In this way they were carried through those awful first weeks and months, until they could become established on their own.

The biggest problems were the legal battles. Jacob and George spent more and more time in trying to forestall new laws being made, that would limit the freedoms of the Mennonites and Jews, in particular. The Mennonites had settled in an area of Altona called Freiheit, or freedom, which was supposed to mean freedom to manufacture and trade as they wished. When other merchants and factory owners found out about the industriousness of the Mennonites, they petitioned their city and town officials to make laws protecting them from the stiff competition provided by the newcomers. It was exactly these new laws that the Mennonite leaders were seeking to have taken away, for they were effective in stalling the expansion plans for the wagon factory to include farm equipment. No permit could be obtained from the Hamburg council to begin this expansion, for the guilds that manufactured horse-drawn plows, harrows and rakes did not welcome competition from the Mennonites.

Jacob realized that Hamburg was a city-state, independent of Holstein, so he went directly to Count von Schauenburg, because Altona was in Holstein. This official was glad to accommodate him, and soon he had the necessary permit to manufacture the implements in Altona. The problem now would be marketing. They could not market them through the Hanseatic League dealers in Hamburg, who boycotted their products. The cloth traders were facing similar restrictions in their area. To make matters worse, the war was once more moving eastwards, this time along the Baltic Sea coast. The Swedes were attacking what had been Danish territory, and the Danes were counter-attacking the Swedes. The religious war of the past decade, which had pitted Catholic against Protestant, had turned to a dispute over territory and trading revenues, fought by two Protestant kingdoms. The Catholics came along behind and mopped up after the Protestants had wrought havoc with each other and with everything in their path. New markets would have to be found for their products, if their industry was going to survive.

Jacob's Aunt Leah's grandson, David Gerbrandt, had just arrived from Holland, where his family had sought refuge from the destruction of Wuestenfelde, and he suggested to Jacob that they try to sell their equipment in Holland. Some of it might need to be adapted somewhat for the type of farming conditions in the polders that were just beginning to be developed there, but there should be a good market. He acted as agent for the factory, and with great difficulty, a few implements found their way to the Netherlands, where they were soon put to active use. Other markets were also opening, but the difficulty of getting items through enemy lines was great, and half the shipments ended up in the hands of Catholic soldiers. Since they had no use for farm implements, they simply stacked them where they would rust away. On a couple of occasions, David actually found piles of their impounded implements and was able to abscond with them for eventual sale.

Market gardens were springing up in the vicinity of Hamburg, largely to feed the burgeoning population in the largest city in northern

Europe at the time. Some of the equipment had been created to meet the needs for these recent developments. Since the farms were outside the city limits, the laws limiting their sale in Hamburg could be ignored outside the city. Soon an increasing number of implements of all kinds were being ordered by prosperous farmers who were converting grain fields to row crops. In return, the Mennonites were receiving more of those crops in return for their implements, thus helping them to develop some stores for the coming winter. Some of the men were busy building root cellars and storage sheds, where the foodstuffs could be kept. Recent immigrants from Holland had also remembered that there were greenhouses in their former homeland, and they served a useful purpose in getting seedling plants going for early transplanting. Some even used them to grow vegetables indoors through the summer, protected from storms and strong winds. Women were busy drying, salting and fermenting the vegetables, in order that they might be kept through the winter months.

Those who had gone out with whaling boats returned occasionally with their catch, and the oil provided a handy income for the community, as well. Profits from the various enterprises were shared quite equally among the Mennonites, administered by the community leaders, who formed a bank to hold the funds in trust. This fund could be utilized for community-approved projects and ventures, which might help the fund to grow, or might deplete it, depending on the success or failure of the venture. The hard work of all caused almost all the ventures to succeed above expectations. Even the elderly were looked after through this fund, if they had no family to care for them. A primitive hospital was organized in a vacant building, where emergencies were taken in for treatment that was sometimes a bit brutal, as the case was during the 17th century. Since there was no trained doctor among them, and no nurse with experience, they were dependent on the experience of a few people that had treated various illnesses and injuries in the past. Most notable among these was the recognized Traichtmoacha (literally Zurechtmacher in High German – right maker), who set bones and manipulated spines and muscles, much as modern chiropractors do, but working on all joints and all limbs, as well as backs.

George Toews came up with the idea first. He brought it to the leaders, who discussed it at length. They thought it had merit, though it was risky. The competition in that area of production was fierce, but it was also possible that it would be very profitable. There was no way to judge it beforehand; they would simply have to begin and see what would come of it. George soon had a couple of men working on obtaining the necessary items they would need, and he went to the town council of Altona himself, to see about getting a permit. The men thought it was a worthwhile enterprise, as all the religions accepted it as part of daily life, so there was no problem in getting the permit. Soon a building was found, and the equipment arrived. The first attempts would be fairly modest, but, if their product was of good quality, it would soon pay for itself, and they would be able to expand with larger equipment, allowing more production. Soon, the thirst of hundreds of Altona's hard-working men and women was being provided for by its first brewery. As they practiced their home-honed skills in brewing beer, the men soon became more expert in their new venture, and the quality of their product was equal to those of the breweries in the big city next door. A new addition to the wagon factory was the production of casks, in which the refreshment was sold. The Mennonites had once more found a way to make their way in a strange place.

Chapter 6

The days grew into weeks and into months. The wagon and cask factory, with the addition of coffins - blacksmith shop was going quite well, the spinning and weaving was picking up, even the whaling had brought in some valuable cash, as well as plenty of lamp oil for the winter. The second planting in the gardens had brought in an unexpected amount of fava beans, which had been dried to provide nourishing food. Winter was now upon them, and the Mennonites had been able to lay up enough in stores to carry them through, if they were very careful.

Count Ernst von Schauenburg didn't see it coming. King Christian IV, who was also Duke of Holstein, demanded a large number of soldiers for his retaliation against Sweden. The count wanted to protect the Mennonites, whom he knew were pacifists and would resist going to war at all. He did the only thing he could do, and that was to enact a law demanding a head tax in lieu of military service. The tax would go toward recruiting mercenaries from other German areas to his county. In the months since the Mennonites had fled Wuestenfelde and settled in Altona, they had proven themselves worthy settlers in the Count's domain, and he wished to keep them there.

The Mennonites didn't see it coming, either. When the Count delivered his demand to George Toews, he took it to the community council and presented it to the men. As they contemplated what this would mean for their ever growing community, they counted up how much the military tax would be – a horrendous sum. It would eat up everything they had saved in order to provide for their people over the next winter, and it would prevent their enlarging the wagon factory. There seemed no way out of the demand, but there seemed also to be no way they could meet it. Then, as if a light had gone on in a dark room, Jacob had an idea. He asked whether he could be excused, and went boldly to the Count's palace.

As he stood at the door awaiting the butler to open, he suddenly realized how brazen it would appear, for him to come as he did to speak to the Count. Still, he somehow believed that his idea was of God, and he stayed, even though something inside him was telling him to run. The door opened, and he asked the man whether it would be possible to speak briefly and privately with the Count. The butler bowed politely and stated that the Count was dining, but he would see. In a few moments, he returned to say that the Count would interrupt his dinner for a short time, and he escorted the visitor into the nearby parlor and bade him be seated. Jacob wondered how best to formulate his request, for it was a request more so than a plan.

"Herr Derksen, it gives me great pleasure to see you here," the Count stated politely, as Jacob rose to greet his superior with a polite bow and handshake. "What brings you here so soon after my rather impolite visit to you this afternoon?"

"Sir, I have a suggestion as to how the Mennonites could pay the military tax, and I wanted to discuss it with you."

"Well, I haven't much time, so please get right to the point, if you would," returned the dignitary.

"It came to me as our community council was discussing how to meet your demand, for we, as you are aware, do not have a great deal of savings, having just fled our home area," Jacob began thoughtfully, and then he gained confidence and continued quite rapidly, "but God has been good, and we have been able to begin some manufacturing that is bringing in enough to keep us alive. A recent development for us, however, might be of interest to you, in regards to your demand for a military tax. Our brewery has just begun production on a larger scale, and the sales are quite good. Apparently our beer has just the right flavor for the people in Altona, and quite a few in Hamburg are also buying it. The thought that came to me was that you might wish to take payment for the military tax in beer, which you could use to recruit soldiers to your county. I believe you mentioned that you would use the tax money for that purpose, and this would possibly serve your purposes just as well. It would certainly be the least difficult way for us to pay what we owe you. And may I tell you, please, our people sincerely appreciate the way in which you and your officials have taken us into your area and made it possible for us to survive and to keep our faith."

"Now that is a novel idea. I find it interesting, I must admit. Please allow me to think about it for a day or two, and I will let you know," the Count responded quite warmly. Then he bade Jacob leave, so that he could return to his dinner. Jacob left with a light heart and a spring in his step. The community council was still discussing the possible ways in which they might raise the outrageous sum, when Jacob walked in. His smile captured their gaze immediately, and George asked him to explain what he had been up to. Jacob's smile grew wider as he returned to his chair and sat down, looking at one after another of the men around the table.

"I visited the Count just now," he began, "and asked him whether we could pay our military tax in beer instead of gold." A gasp was multiplied by as many times as there were men around the table.

"Was he interested?" asked George.

"He said he would think about it for a day or so, and then he would let us know. The idea was a bit novel, he said, but he was not immediately against it. I suggest we pray that he will accept it."

That seemed a bit of a novel idea to the group, as well, but the men quickly agreed that this was a matter for earnest prayer. The community council knelt over their chairs as Jacob led them in a supplication that God would cause the Count to accept their abundant beer instead of their meager gold. At that, the men got up and went to their homes.

When Jacob got to the house, he found a cold supper on the table, with his family already in bed. With an inner peace he bowed his head and thanked the Lord for the blessings of the day, and eating the food quickly, he also prepared for bed, suddenly feeling the tiredness that follows such exhilaration. Rebekah was in bed, but her discomfort because of the baby inside her made sleeping rather a chore, rather than a rest. Jacob, on the other hand, drifted off into a deep slumber almost immediately that he had lain down.

After his breakfast of cooked oats, which he cooked himself, Jacob left for the wagon factory. He realized that his wife was overexerting herself to keep all their own as well as the Guenther children satisfied, in addition to her normal housework, but he could not do anything about their situation, except to work hard at providing what he could for their needs. He prayed, as he hitched his horse to the carriage, for it was some distance into Altona from where he lived in Hamburg. He prayed that somehow God would bless this somewhat silly idea he had presented to the Count, and that it would be the salvation of the Mennonites in Altona and Hamburg.

He had just gotten going, when Benjamin came running behind him, beckoning him to stop. As the boy puffed up to the carriage, he blurted out, "Come quickly, the baby is coming!"

Jacob gave the reins to Benjamin, ordering him to go for Mrs. Roosen, who was a midwife. The boy sprang into action, proud that his father would entrust the horse and carriage into his hands. With a somewhat grim face, he turned the horse in the direction of the Roosen place and trotted off. Jacob leapt up the steps two at a time and was soon at his wife's side. She was breathing very heavily, and the labor pains were severe. Jacob did what he could to comfort her, as they waited for the midwife to arrive. The baby, however, was not intending to wait until everything was in proper order, before he was in the birth canal, and the labor became very intense. Suddenly, there was a great gush of blood. A hemorrhage! Jacob did what he could to stop the flow of blood, but it was too late. The baby came just then, but Rebekah's life drained from her. In his helplessness, Jacob covered his face with his hands, shook from head to foot, and began to weep. At that moment, he realized that he must do something for the baby, or it would also perish. He did the best he could to get it cleaned up and breathing, and when Mrs. Roosen came in, he was holding the little boy in his arms. He had not known how to cut the umbilical cord, so it was still connected to the dead womb. How thankful he was that the woman knew just what to do at this time, and soon he had the baby in his arms, clean, breathing clearly, and crying loudly. She then began to do what she could to clean up the dead woman and the bedroom, though she said she would call on Mrs. Thiessen to come, as she knew better what to do with bodies. She also volunteered to stay and help look after the children, for they were now getting up and getting in the way.

Jacob could not remember later how he got through the next few days. It seemed like a nightmare of frustration, rage, weeping, hope and despair. Like soldiers, each emotion in turn invaded his mind and body, and left him disoriented and fragile. Mrs. Roosen stayed with him and the children, in order to keep things in order. Because her husband had died some months before in an accident at work, she knew something about what Jacob was going through. Patiently she dealt with his tantrums and his depression, while keeping a close eye on the children. She had two children herself, a son of 16 named Gerritt, after his father, and a daughter of 15, Elizabeth, who was usually just called Lizzy. This made it easier to distinguish her from Jacob's daughter of 8 years, who went by Elizabeth. That somewhat filled the house, for there were now two independent adults and 12 children, made up of three families.

Both Jacob and Martina Roosen knew that others were talking about them. It was not considered proper to have a strange woman in the house, even when it was necessary, as the present case definitely was. There was nothing about Martina that attracted Jacob to her, for she was quite large and masculine-looking, with a large square face with tiny eyes and a very small mouth, but a large flat nose. Her voice, however, was high-pitched, asthmatic and wheezy, and seemed forced each time she spoke. Her appearance belied her real interests and abilities, which were academic and scientific. She, however, had a great heart for the children. There was nothing about Jacob that attracted Martina to him, for he was balding and almost gaunt from overwork. His beard was somewhat unkempt and graying at the corners. His eyes showed the stress that he was under. She was a widow who needed someone to care for her, so she couldn't be fussy. Jacob had suddenly been widowed with a large family to care for, and this woman was willing to accept the responsibility. He was able to put her and her two children, as well as baby Jacob IV, into the small apartment connected with his house, which gave them a bit of privacy from him, but no privacy at all for each other. With a shrug of the shoulders, each of them accepted what appeared to be the inevitable.

Jacob knew that the elder of the Mennonites would be visiting from Prussia within the next few days, so he simply told Martina at supper that they would "take care of their business" when he was present. Martina nodded, knowing in her heart what that "business" was. They needed each other, and that was sufficient grounds to marry. Neither could consider love to be part of the equation, but both felt deeply, that love, or at least mutual respect, would grow out of their new relationship. That gave hope. They went to the Altona Standesamt, the place where civil weddings were registered, and completed the formalities there together with their combined families, so that they were legally married. Since there was nothing left to move, and nowhere to go for a honeymoon, and with children all around them, they realized that their marriage would be one of necessity only.

Elder Peters came, the church wedding was held in their home, without special wedding garments. Martina moved into Jacob's room with him, and the children's quarters were re-arranged, so that the apartment was given to the boys – Gerritt, Benjamin, Joshua, Nicholas and Jonathan – while the rest of the group was placed into rooms in the main part of the house, girls sharing with girls, and Willy and Jacob IV, called JJ for short, in the nursery. In this way, life continued for all of them. There was no joy, as both were still grieving, and the children picked up on this, becoming whiny and morose.

Jacob continued to oversee the wagon factory but declined to preach, he had one or another of the deacons preach, so that he could find time for his other responsibilities, and so that he could deal with his sense of loss and abandonment. In the wrenching personal circumstances he had just gone through, he was not aware that Count von Schauenburg had come to George and had accepted his proposal to take the tax in beer instead of money. When he was made aware of that, he rejoiced with the others, that they would continue to be able to worship as they felt God's Word taught them to, and that their young men would not have to go off to those senseless wars. He also realized that a major part of their revenues was now simply going into this tax, which was plainly extortion. Little did Jacob know that this would, for many years into the future, become a haunting part of the Mennonites' life. "The Lord giveth, and the Lord taketh away" came to his mind many times in those days.

Martina did her best to cope with the many children that her marriage had suddenly made her the mother of, but, because she was not naturally a good mother, but rather an intellectual person and a student, her nature was somewhat stern, and Jacob's children were not accustomed to a mother whose reaction to the stress was to strike out verbally against whatever annoyed her. It took a few weeks of stressful engagement, before she was able to establish herself as the new matron of the house, especially with Benjamin and Joshua. Susan, who was the oldest of the Guenther children, also had some problems adjusting to this third mother in her young life. The younger ones were not affected by this so much, as they were still learning what socialization was all about, so this seemed natural to them.

Gerritt Roosen, for he kept his surname, was precocious. He had learned to read almost by himself, and he excelled in all matters of schooling. It was obvious to Jacob, as it had been to Martina that he must be sent to Latin school to get an education. Although this was not common among Mennonites, exceptions were occasionally made. The danger of losing a soul to the "devil" through the worldly ideas of the educated people was just too great, so most Mennonites preferred that their young people not be exposed to such temptations. Martina had heard that there was such a school near her old house, in the direction of the center of the city, so she set about sending Gerritt on a search for it. Within an hour he had found the school, which was within walking distance of their present house. He could attend from home, which pleased Jacob and Martina very much, and Gerritt, too. He could begin right away and hopefully catch up with the others in his age group, for there was no way to measure where his learning had taken him, though the Headmaster was very impressed with the obvious abilities of the young man. He had tested very well in all subject areas. As he started, it became very evident quite quickly that this gifted young man was going to develop into an extraordinary scholar.

Benjamin, on the other hand, was more practically inclined, as his mother had been, so he had no desire to go to higher schools. Instead, he was finishing his elementary school with the goal of becoming a carpenter like his father. He showed no inclination to become a preacher. His greatest joy would be to become a worker in the wagon factory.

The girls were as different as night and day, too. Lizzy was interested in becoming a doctor. Her father's death had increased this interest in her, and she was finishing her last public school year with the thought of further studies at the Latin school, too, in preparation for university studies in medicine. Because she was Martina's natural child, her mother tended to favor her. Mary, by contrast, wanted to work with children. Her goal was to become a teacher, like her grandmother had been. The younger children still had a different goal each time they were asked, depending on the events that were shaping their days at the moment.

By the time the school year had come to an end, all the children had demonstrated their best efforts in whatever subject interested them most. Where Benjamin excelled in mathematics and science, Gerritt was best in German, Latin, French, English and history. He loved literature, and he had demonstrated an amazing ability as a writer and orator. Lizzy was good in sciences, particularly biology, and Mary was demonstrating that she had a good command of the skills learned in elementary school. The younger children were working diligently under Martina's watchful and stern eye, to learn the basic skills that would make them successful later. Although she was an apt student herself, she was not gifted with the communication skills to teach the skills she herself knew so well.

Jacob and Martina tried hard to make their marriage successful. Each was conscious of the other's needs, and each was desperately in need emotionally and spiritually. Each had suffered immeasurable loss in a sudden, cataclysmic way, and both were still grieving that loss deeply. Because of the circumstances of their marriage, they had nothing to grab hold of that would allow them to build their relationship with one another. As a result, each day became like a machine. It started with work, it continued with work, and at night it shut down, even though there was still a lot of unfinished work. They maintained a respectful politeness toward each other, mainly because of the children, but there was no spark, no hint of deep love in their relationship.

Although he could do his work in the wagon factory without feeling it draining his energies, Jacob was well aware of the impact this was having on his ministry as a deacon in the church. He felt self-conscious and hypocritical when he was counseling someone. Eventually, he simply told the other deacons that he could no longer continue in this role. They understood, but tried to convince him that this was just a phase in his grieving, that it would go away with time. Jacob was adamant, however; he wanted to discard this responsibility. He was found after that, not sitting any more at the front of the church, but seeking out the back-most seats for his family.

Martina had the daily housework to occupy her mind. Because of the number and ages of the children, this amounted to a monumental task each day, so she had no time to brood on her situation. To be sure, Jacob was a good husband in many ways. He did not scold her or belittle her, as many men did to their wives. Nor did he miss complimenting her on a good meal or a nice piece of clothing she had made for one of the children. Still, she missed the intimacy of a good marriage. Jacob was merely a professional house-husband to her, and she was simply a not-too-professional housewife to him. Martina could only be satisfied that she was not mistreated, and that her basic needs were being met. Sexual relationship had been attempted, but after the first unsuccessful night, all attempts had ceased entirely. The little things that lovers do to show each other their feelings for one another were non-existent. Life continued as an unstoppable machine, without excitement and without change. Dreariness, and eventually a mild depression, set in for both of them.

Chapter 7

The Mennonite Church was not finished with divisions when the Guenthers and others perished in the Plague epidemic. Traveling preachers came around every so often, and it seemed that each had a unique understanding of the doctrines that made up the Mennonite faith. There were many things on which all agreed – baptism on confession of faith as an adult, a requirement of baptism for church membership, communion in both kinds for all church members, the supremacy of God's Word over traditions and popes, the privilege of believers to read and interpret God's Word for themselves, non-resistance in any form of confrontation, refusal to participate in government, or even the taking of an oath of allegiance, and a strict separation from all things worldly. The freedom of each believer to interpret God's Word for himself or herself led to many points of division, as one preacher took one aspect further than the other, while the other emphasized another point. This was especially applied to the area of separation from the world, but it was also applied to other doctrinal issues, such as the nature of Jesus Christ.

One speaker gave a thundering declaration that the only biblical mode of baptism was by immersion, and another gave historical evidence for baptism by sprinkling or by pouring. One thought that all prayers should be uttered audibly, especially those offered in public worship, while another would only accept silent prayer as representing the true personal nature of prayer in the closet, as it were. One considered foot-washing to be obligatory on Christians, especially before taking communion, while another thought of it as only symbolic of the Christian's need to be humble and to have a serving attitude to others. The local deacons were torn between this teaching and that, and they constantly had to take a stand on one item or another, which divided the church internally, if not visibly. Because Jacob had removed himself from his position in the church, he was spared the tedious discussions, but one or another of the local leaders was constantly coming to him for advice, recognizing his long service to the congregation. Jacob, because of his personal troubles, was not always able to give objective advice to those that came to him. Slowly, he sank into a deeper depression, which eventually made it difficult for him to carry on in the wagon factory. It affected his life at home, where his responses were mostly mono-syllabic and curt. More and more was being thrust on Martina, who was finding the care of twelve children and her depressed husband to be more than she could manage. She was becoming sterner every day, scolding about things that were quite normal in children's play, simply because they annoyed her. She wished for total silence, and that could not be expected in such a household. The older children, who were both her own, were somewhat helpful, but they lacked experience, and she did not have time to teach them. She simply expected too much of them. That caused them to resent her demands, and then, in retaliation for her lack of appreciation, they did not do as well as they might have on the various assigned chores. Jacob would then come into the picture and ban any activity at all, banishing everyone to his or her bedroom to allow for a bit of quiet. He did not allow his passions to get the best of him, to the point of beating any of them, but he sometimes administered corporal punishment quite severely, especially on the younger ones.

JJ suffered the most through this. As a newborn baby being raised by someone that was not his mother, he was helpless to affect the situation. Instead, he became the victim of the tension in the home. He cried almost constantly. This added to the tension, and drove both Jacob and Martina further into their individual depressions. That exacerbated their negative behavioral patterns, and they became even stricter and more vocal in their attacks on the children.

Leah and Heinrich Gerbrandt had had one daughter who was similar in age to Jacob, and she came to visit her cousin. How she got through enemy lines to Hamburg was a mystery that all marvelled at, but she showed up at their place one day. Dorcas Gerbrandt, for she had never married, was somewhat of a Dorfschwester – a village nurse – who volunteered her time to care for needs within the village. In her case, her efforts had been used within the Mennonite Community in Wuestenfelde until the army made its approach. In the confusion that ensued in trying to get everyone out of the village, she got separated from the wagons that were heading south, and she had ended in Luebeck instead of Altona. In the months that followed, she found work in private homes, nursing older family members in Lutheran homes. When she heard that the rest of her family had gotten to Altona, she determined to visit them there. It appeared that God was guiding her to her cousin's house at just the right time, for both Jacob and Martina were at their lowest ebb.

As Dorcas listened first to Jacob, then to Martina, describing their situation, she realized that she would not be able to leave quickly. This would be a long-term project, and it would take all her energies and wisdom, gathered through many situations in many homes. She saw a few things that needed immediate attention, and got the older children to accompany her in getting those out of the way. Because she worked with them, the young people learned quickly and soon the jobs were done that had lain undone for days. She assessed JJ's situation, and together with Lizzy, she was able to establish a routine for his feedings, baths and general care. She taught Lizzy how to make the formula that was necessary, as mother's milk was not available, and how to use her finger to get JJ to suck, so that he got his nourishment easily. That brought some measure of order to the household. Jacob and Martina sat and watched what was happening, too overwhelmed by their own woes, and too absorbed in their individual pathos, to really appreciate what was happening before them, but getting evermore relaxed as things seemed to become more peaceful around them.

Sorting out the children by their family roots took some time, but Dorcas tried to see each child as an individual, without specific family attachments. Each one needed to be treated specially in her mind, and she found ways quite soon to accomplish some aspects of this. That, in turn, won them over for her instruction and occasional reprimands, when they failed to live up to what she was trying to teach them about living together in a blended family.

Finding a place for her in the crowded house was taken care of by moving Agnes in with the older girls and Willy with the older boys. JJ still had a crib in his parents' room. That freed up one small room for Dorcas. She had not brought very much with her, so some things had to be found for her to wear. Because they had not yet had time to dispose of Rebekah's things, they found enough clothing for her to wear.

To see his cousin wearing his deceased wife's clothes had a strange effect on Jacob. It actually brought out some of his former character, and he began to be his old self fairly quickly after that. Soon he was back to his work at the wagon factory. The men had graciously held his place for him as their leader. One of the men had filled in temporarily, but he gladly stepped back to his old work once Jacob arrived back at work. Jacob, in turn, recognized the ability of that one, and he promoted him to be the foreman to take care of many of the things he had normally done.

The school year finished, and Benjamin, now thirteen years old and finished elementary school, was incorporated into the wagon shop, to learn the trade from his father and the other men. Gerritt found work with some weavers, which he especially enjoyed. He was even allowed to accompany the agent who was selling their cloth on several occasions, and he enjoyed this aspect of it especially. Lizzy was needed at home, but Jacob arranged that she should be paid a small wage for her work, so that she also felt that she was earning something, and certainly under Dorcas's practiced guidance, she learned a great deal. Joshua, Mary, Susan, Elizabeth and Jonathan were put to work tending the family garden plot, which seemed always to need weeding or watering.

All of this helped Martina's spirits to revive, as well. Soon she lost her forlorn look and began to help out in the house, especially in the care of JJ. That lightened Dorcas's load considerably, and the two women occasionally found time to sit together and chat over some sewing or knitting. On sunny days they could be seen outside, doing whatever work they could bring with them. The sun had a brightening effect on each one's spirits, and by the end of the summer, both Jacob and Martina had largely recovered their former energies. There was still no sign of affection between them, but they tolerated each other much more easily. That brought a greater measure of peace to the household, and things took on a routine that was more productive and congenial.

The devil is not unaware of the moments when he can attack us more easily, and that proved to be the next problem for Jacob and the Mennonites. Jacob had once more been co-opted into the community council, and he was again involved in the deliberations involving the Mennonites. Because of pressures resulting from the religious war that moved about around them, the city council in Hamburg announced that no religious services of any kind, other than the prescribed Lutheran or Catholic ones, could be held within the city. That resulted in some Mennonites and Jews from the city coming to share in the services being held in Altona. Since both groups were using the same building, that burst the seams of the small structure. They were both left looking for a larger place in which to worship. The only one available was the wagon factory, which once again had to be cleared every Friday evening, to make a place for the Jewish worship on the Sabbath, and for the Mennonite service on Sunday. Then, every Monday morning it had to be gotten ready for production again. To be sure, some items, such as the forge or the large chain hoist could not be moved, so the service took place around them. Jacob was once more under pressure to care for the needs of his people. It took some months before he was asked to preach again, and he refused, but the deacons continued to ask that he return to his job as their pastor.

Martina realized that she was doomed to be the mother of a dozen children, most of whom were not her own. The implications of this had not fully dawned on her, as she had accepted marriage as a way out of her personal crisis as a widow among refugees. Dorcas was able to draw her out occasionally, to determine what her feelings were, so that she could offer suitable counselling and practical help. She found out that Martina was actually more of an intellectual than a practical woman with domestic skills. Her rather plain looks belied the intellect that was struggling to free itself from the chains of her circumstances. It was then that Dorcas realized that her duties at the Derksen household would not be ending at all. She accepted her role as the household manager graciously, for her calling, she felt, was to meet the needs within the village, and this was the need before her.

One evening, after a particularly good day for both Jacob and Martina, she broached the subject to them. "I would like to thank both of you for taking me into your family as you have done. You have been very gracious, and both of you seemed to need some help when I came. I have been noticing some things during this time, though, and I think I can help you further, if you wish."

"What do you have in mind?" queried Martina.

"I believe that you would really rather be reading and writing, than looking after children all the time," began Dorcas diplomatically, looking Martina in the eye. "I think you are frustrated by the amount of time it takes to care for such a large family, and then you get overwhelmed by it all."

"We married each other, because we both needed each other," Jacob chimed in.

"Yes, that is true. You were both left alone with your children, and no mate to help you. It seemed a good idea to marry and share your load. The problem was that the load was too heavy for both of you. The load I am talking about was not the size of the washing, or the amount of money needed to raise that many children. It was the mental load of planning the day-to-day work, the pressure of trying to balance all the responsibilities at one time," continued Dorcas. "Jacob, you have come from a line of people that cares about others, sometimes more so than about yourselves. I share that heritage, and I think it comes from God. The war has made it necessary for us all to move, and Mennonites in particular are being attacked, because we refuse to fight for either side in the battles. Wuestenfelde was leveled, I am told, because the Catholic armies were not paid, so they pillaged villages to stay alive. That is still happening all around us. Martina told me that even your gardens had been pillaged here. Then, both of you lost your loved ones suddenly, and you were left even more destitute than you had been before. It is no wonder that your nerves collapsed."

Jacob marveled that his cousin had such a grasp on the entirety of the situation. He remained silent, contemplating the gravity of what she had said.

"Why does God do this to us?" Martina exploded, her high-pitched, wheezing voice rising even higher than usual. "We never get any peace. As long as we keep up this idea that we are doing what He wants by being so different, we are hounded by everyone else. Can't we just quietly believe what we think is right, without making a scene before everyone else?"

Jacob was about to pounce on her with a long harangue about their beliefs, but he caught the eye of Dorcas, who squinted slightly and moved her head from side to side just a little to indicate that he should forbear. He absorbed himself by swatting at a mosquito flying near him.

"Yes, when we believe something as deep as the Bible teaches us, we place our lives on the line for our beliefs, and that causes those around us, who believe differently, to distrust us, or even to hate us. Then they find ways to attack us. Jesus said that in this world His disciples would suffer persecution, so we shouldn't be surprised when it happens," continued Dorcas carefully, so as not to offend Martina's sensitivities.

"But the Lutherans and Catholics claim they worship the same God we do. Even the Jews claim the same. How do we know that we have the one and only truth, that all of us should believe? Now the city council has ordered us not to have services in Hamburg anymore. What does that say about us in this world?" continued Martina in her rebellious vein. Both Jacob and Dorcas could see at this point what Martina's deepest problem really was, something she had kept to herself through all the difficulties she had borne.

Jacob leaned back in his chair and stroked his beard thoughtfully. Dorcas sat stone-still on her chair and watched Martina's huge face move in the contortions of deep thought.

"We live by faith," began Jacob tentatively, "the world around has adopted a system of worship that fits into their culture, rather than allowing their worship to mold their culture."

"That's right," chimed in Dorcas, "we look into God's Word and find out how we should live, rather than looking into it to find phrases that support our convoluted ideas about life. The other churches have basically followed the traditions of the past in their worship. The Lutherans changed a few things about those beliefs, but it didn't change their lives. It changed their politics. The German princes didn't want to pay their tithes to Rome anymore, so they adopted Lutheranism as a way of getting out of that burden. They can choose which faith their region will hold. Otherwise, they are all Germans or Dutchmen, or whatever, and live like all others around them do. Their faith has done nothing to change their lives. They drink too much, they fight with each other, they try to find ways of defrauding each other without being caught, and they swear terribly, but they are 'good Christians,' if they go to church regularly and pay their tithes to their Church. We Mennonites believe that we should live out what the Bible teaches, and it teaches us that we should not take the sword, but should love one another, and we should not swear at all."

"I guess you are right, but it seems to me that we would all live a lot more comfortably, if we didn't carry our religion quite so far, so that we even look different from the people around us." Martina was quite reflective now, musing about some of the other issues connected with their faith that were bothering her. "For instance, what do we accomplish by looking so old-fashioned? Some of our people won't even wear buttons, saying that they are ostentatious, but use only hooks and eyes, as if that system were given us in the Bible. We can't wear any colors, so we all look like drab old hags. And doing our hair in a bun only adds to this."

"I guess we'll just have to look to our pastors, elders and deacons for the answer to that," laughed Dorcas, noticing that Jacob winced at hearing Martina's criticism, and being well aware that she was wearing her hair in a bun, just to keep it out of her way as she worked.

"Our church council will discuss it again, but it has been part of every discussion we have had for the past century, and I don't think it will change soon," replied Jacob grimly. One of the tenets of Menno's teachings had been that God's people were required to dress modestly and avoid ostentation in every form, especially in their appearance, for that was worldly, so the practice had been laid down quite early, that all must dress and appear somewhat out of fashion, as a statement to the world around that they were seeking to follow the dictates of God's Word.

"I believe we have a bit of that new drink that the Turks have been using for centuries, don't we?" Jacob changed the subject. "I would really like a good warm cup of coffee with some cream just now."

All agreed that this would be a fitting conclusion to the evening's discussion, and Dorcas went off to the kitchen stove to prepare it.

Dick Derksen

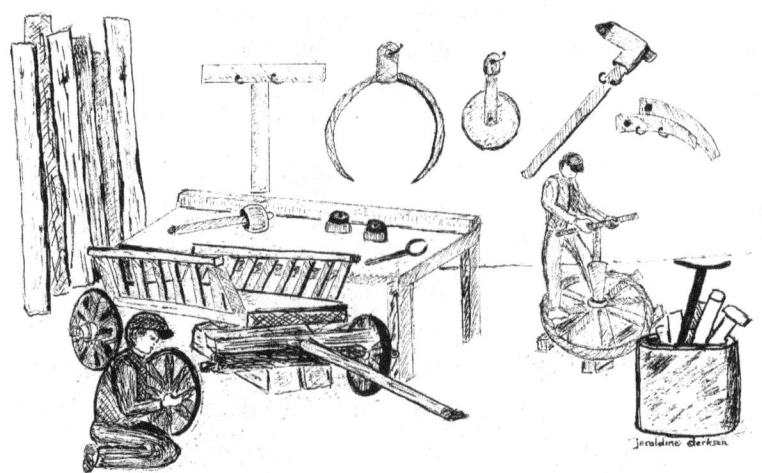

Wagon Factory in Altona

Chapter 8

"What are you going to do about it?" Martina's whine was almost more than Jacob could bear.

"There isn't anything we can do about it," Jacob retorted.

"But it's going to tear apart our church," Martina was not going to give up easily. "We've already got five families going to services separately from ours, and more are talking about it."

"They think they have more of the Truth than we have, so anything we say is shoved back at us with the statement that we are not following God's Word as closely as they are."

Jacob knew all about the problem. He and the deacons had talked about it among themselves, and they had confronted the leaders of the insurgent group, but all to no avail. It is difficult to convince someone who believes he has more of the Truth than you have, that you are more right than he is. The split-off group was still deeply Mennonite in its leanings, except that they emphasized baptism by immersion, which earned them the Dutch appellative 'Dompelaars," or Dunkers. They also practiced taking communion only in the evening, as the Last Supper had been in the gospels. They believed you needed an experience of salvation that was clear and singular, and that you could have assurance of salvation from that moment.

"Maybe you need to call for the Elder to come and talk to them," suggested Dorcas.

That seemed a practical idea, and Jacob acknowledged that it might be necessary. He would see the others on the church council tomorrow, and they would send someone to find Elder Janzen. This could prove an elusive chase, for the Elder traveled extensively, sometimes in Friesland, other times in Holstein or Lower Saxony, and sometimes even as far away as Prussia. Though the Mennonites had a council of deacons in every congregation, they did have an Elder who oversaw all the churches in a large area, performed baptisms, weddings and funerals, and arbitrated the many issues that seemed to come up all the time and everywhere.

"This isn't the first, nor will it likely be the last, church split among the Mennonites. Because of our belief that everyone can interpret the scriptures for themselves, once they have believed in Jesus Christ for salvation and been baptized in whatever way their church does it and have thus become members of the Mennonite church, we cannot forbid anyone from following their interpretation, even if it is different from the main church body's inclinations. The group that had supported the Guenthers was a recent example of that. In their case, sober second thought following the punishing Plague brought them back into the fold, though not without some misgivings. Perhaps this group will also return in repentance," continued Jacob thoughtfully. "The prophet Jeremiah said something about this, too. 'Stand ye in the ways, and see, and ask for the old paths, where is the good way, and walk therein, and ye shall find rest for your souls.'"

"Yes, and in the meantime we look like fools before the Lutherans and Catholics around us. They have their beliefs sent down from above, and no one is allowed to interpret the Bible apart from what the Church teaches. In fact, the Catholics aren't even allowed to own Bibles, and very few Lutherans have one," Martina retorted. She had done some research into this, it seemed.

"If we do look like fools to them, it hasn't stopped an occasional one in either group from becoming a Mennonite," Jacob responded. "Some people recognize the fallacy of believing what their Church teaches, for they have seen where it leads. It seems to be totally political, and that has led to this war we are in right now. For the common parishioner, there doesn't seem to be much to show for belonging to the Church – no change of life, no assurance of salvation, no access to the Word of God for themselves, nothing for children once they are baptized, and no help against the onslaughts of the war. There is only the liturgical form of worship that is repeated every Sunday. We just interviewed a couple that lost their son in the war, fighting as a mercenary in the Catholic army, even though they are Lutherans. It seems that the Danes shot one of their own believers, who was fighting on the other side. There is no reason to this awful conflict, and neither side will give in, because it is no longer about belief, but about power and territory. No one will win: everyone will lose. This country is being laid waste all around us. The couple could see that our belief in non-resistance made much more sense than their penchant for war."

For the first time since their marriage, Jacob and Martina were having an extended conversation. Until this time, conversation, if any, was mostly in monosyllables and dealing with immediate issues of the home and family. As Jacob reflected on this, he came to the realization that this woman had a very good intellect, and that she meant well for him and the Mennonite community. Even though her disheveled appearance caused him to shrink back from liking her, a certain admiration seemed appropriate.

Elder Janzen, when he was found by the delegate, came at once. This was not the first of the Dompelaar offshoots from the old church, and he had had to deal with similar situations almost everywhere. The people seemed well-meaning in their beliefs. They based everything clearly on biblical teachings, and that very literally. Such a group could not easily be persuaded to return to the old ways of the central Mennonite church. But, as he had tried elsewhere, he would try to convince the leaders of the group that their divisiveness was not a biblical trait. Perhaps this group would hear him out and return, but he had his doubts.

In the meantime, Martina left more and more of the work to Dorcas, as she sought to get involved in other activities that stimulated her intellect and her personal interests. Her children were in school, and only the younger Derksen and Guenther ones remained at home during the day, so she was often found walking about town, either in Hamburg or in Altona, speaking with this one and that, and frequenting the libraries of priests, pastors and monasteries. She read voraciously, especially in areas of theology and history, but also in general literature, both in German and in Dutch. There was a newssheet, the beginnings of a city newspaper, which came out twice a week and was distributed in both Hamburg and Altona, and this became a favorite pastime. Because of this, she was more aware of what went on around the city and the town than the other Mennonites. She often commented on happenings at the supper table, as all of them gathered around the long table. Her own children, being the oldest in the combined family, were very interested in what she had found out, and Jacob and Dorcas appreciated being brought up to the moment on the news.

Dorcas bore the extra work patiently, realizing that she had become the mother to her cousin's children, both those born to Rebekah and those adopted from the Guenthers. Hers was not to know the secrets of politics and armies; hers was to manage a household and express Christian love to her charges, and express it she did. Her efforts in cooking, baking, and preserving of food resulted in a full cellar before the coming winter. She sewed, mended, and altered clothing for the children and for Jacob. She avoided making anything for Martina, for she could not make herself like this strange woman. She was so different from other Mennonite women; she didn't fit into any mold that Dorcas had seen among Lutherans in Luebeck, either. She was unique to herself, so Dorcas, because of her total lack of understanding of such a personality, simply ignored her.

The Dompelaars didn't go away. They continued to meet separately and to draw away some of the most devout of the Mennonites from the main group. There were people in the group from every enterprise the Mennonites had set up, so it was not possible to isolate the one group from the other. What did happen was that ordinary conversations turned to theological topics, and that challenged everyone to think more deeply about their own beliefs, and to compare them to those of the others and to the Bible itself.

Jacob overheard one such conversation as his men were assembling wagons one day.

"We take communion in the evening, because Jesus introduced it at the Last Supper before He was taken and crucified," said Isaac Funk, for he had gone over to the group.

"But Jesus Himself said that, 'whenever' we take the bread or the cup, we should do it in remembrance of Him. That means it can be celebrated at any time, not just evenings. It should be celebrated by the church whenever it chooses to meet, not necessarily just in an evening, and not just during the Easter season, when it was introduced by Jesus," another argued. The conversation continued in that vein between grunts connected with the work, but because the work was going on and the conversation was friendly, Jacob saw no need to intervene.

On another occasion the topic was baptism, and this got quite heated for a while, but Jacob held his peace, again because the work was progressing well.

"The only biblical way to be baptized is by immersion, because the Ethiopian went into the water, the Bible says, in order to be baptized," one worker stated.

"If baptism is like being cleansed by the sprinkling of blood, as in the Old Testament, then sprinkling is the way to do it, because we are cleansed by the sprinkling," another objected.

"But Paul says that all the Israelites were baptized in going through the Red Sea, which represents total immersion," another chimed in.

"Peter says something like, 'sprinkling of the blood of Jesus Christ,' and he is referring to those who were 'elect according to the foreknowledge of God,'" another added. "We are God's children, because of His foreknowledge, and we become his children by the sprinkling of water that signifies the cleansing of the blood of Christ, and all of this is by faith in His finished work," that amateur theologian concluded.

"We have plenty of water here to immerse people in, but in some places there wasn't enough, so sprinkling became the popular way of baptizing people," the historian added.

Thus the conversation continued, and thus it would continue for years to come, yea, for centuries to come, as different groups took their cue from different biblical passages and different historical eras.

As suspected by Jacob, Elder Janzen's presence did little to convince the split-away group to return to the old way. They were right, the old group was wrong, and that was enough. Their leaders were godly men who read their Bibles faithfully and who preached effectively. Henceforth there would be two opposing groups of Mennonites in Altona and Hamburg. Although the individuals got along fairly well socially, they could not agree to the others' positions on these topics, so they agreed to go their separate ecclesiastical ways as amicably as possible. That did not, however, stop the household gossips from lacerating each other verbally.

Chapter 9

"I want to leave," Martina said one day, "I want a divorce, so I can go on with my own life."

"But you needed me," said Jacob in surprise, "you couldn't survive without a husband."

"I can find another man, if that is necessary, and I have already arranged to start working in the Hamburg University Library and Bookstore next week. I'll be all right, and my children will do just fine without your strict supervision, too." That last part cut deeply into Jacob's spirit.

"You can't get a divorce unless you can prove that I have been unfaithful to you, and I have not," retorted Jacob.

"I can just leave you and live my own life, then. Even without the papers, I can make a life for myself without you." Martina was becoming more adamant. "You have Dorcas to look after the household, so you will survive. We haven't really been a man and wife from the beginning of our marriage anyway."

Jacob was stunned. How could this woman do such a thing? What should he do? His first instinct was to fight her with every verbal argument he could think of, but he knew in his heart that this would only make her more determined to leave him. Never once did he think that he needed to keep her because of personal need or family need. She had never been close to him, as a wife should be; she had admitted as much. She had not functioned as a mother for a long time, but was drifting farther and farther away from him and from the household chores. His cousin had taken over that role, and that would probably not change. Gerritt and Lizzy would make it on their own, without a father figure. They were extremely intelligent, as their mother was. Jacob recognized this gift in Martina. Gerritt had already become a talking point among the textile merchants, for his insights into that occupation. He was talking about the need for someone to make hosiery and market it, something that was just then coming into vogue.

As he sat looking at the floor, Jacob's shoulders slumped, and he realized he was slumping mentally and emotionally, as well. His nerves were once again giving out on him, and he was settling into his previous depression. Speechless, he drifted down into the darkness of mental fatigue and emotional numbness.

"Jacob, what's the matter with you?" the words brought him to a sudden realization that he was not alone in his dark thoughts, anymore. Startled, he looked up with a jerk to see Dorcas coming through the room with a basket of fresh washing from the garden clothes line. How was he going to tell her the news? What should he tell his children? Jacob struggled with the magnitude of the situation he now faced, for during his lapse, Martina must have packed her things and gone with her children. He looked at the clock on the mantelpiece and realized that he had been in a dozing state for a couple of hours.

"Martina announced that she is leaving me," began Jacob dejectedly. "She must have packed her bags and taken her children out just now."

"She can't do that!" Jacob's cousin showed some of her righteous indignation in her explosion. "Women don't just walk out on their husbands."

"She said she had a job in Hamburg, and that she and the children would do just fine."

"That means, then, that I will have to continue to raise your family." Dorcas was quick to assess the situation.

"I can't expect you to do that, Dorcas, you just happened to come into our family situation at a critical time, and you will want to go about your own things now." Jacob sought to console his cousin, but he realized she was right. He could not seek another woman to be his wife and also to be a father and mother to his extended family, for he was still married to Martina, for love or the lack thereof.

"No, you can't marry again, because your wife is still living, even though she isn't living with you. Mennonites don't seek divorces, unless the partner has been unfaithful, and I doubt that anyone would want to make Martina unfaithful." Dorcas's insight was almost painful, but at the same time, Jacob could not help smiling slightly at the comment. Dorcas had probably guessed that there was no sexual attraction between him and Martina all along. "I will stay. I will be happy to stay. God wants it. I am ready to do what He wants. In a strange way, I love you and all your children very much. I will be your housekeeper and mother-figure to your children, if you will allow me to stay."

Jacob shrugged his shoulders, lifting his arms in resignation, smiled, and relaxed in his chair. "Please make me a cup of coffee," he requested politely, as he settled down against the soft fabric. He watched as Dorcas put down the wash basket and went to the stove to prepare hot water.

Things went fairly well for the next week, as the children were already used to having Dorcas act as their mother, and they accepted her nurturing with love and devotion. It took Benjamin a while longer to seek to understand what had happened, for he was old enough to begin asking questions.

"Father, why did Mother Martina leave us?" he asked one day, as he was helping Jacob rake leaves in the yard.

"She came to us, son, to help with the birth of JJ, when your mother died, and because she had lost her husband shortly before, she stayed to help look after you. It seemed to be the necessary thing to do, and she was free to do so. We both needed each other, even though we were very different types of people," Jacob tried to tell his son as gently as possible, how the situation had developed. "We realized that we were not really suited to each other, but we got married, because both of us needed someone who could meet our needs. She thought she needed a man to care for her and her two children, Gerritt and Lizzy, and I definitely needed a woman to care for you and the other children, especially since JJ was just a newborn baby. We were a big household, and I couldn't work and also care for all of you. You and the others were too young to look after yourselves, so Martina and I decided we should marry, so that she could look after all of you. The problem was that she really couldn't look after all of you. That was not how God made her. She was interested only in reading, learning and talking about new ideas. She was what we call an intellectual, not a practical woman, and she needed that mental stimulation to keep her going. Doing housework didn't provide that kind of satisfaction, so she got depressed. Because she was depressed and couldn't keep up with things, I tried to step in and help out – you'll remember some of my bumbling when I did – and then I got depressed. You will also remember how I got angry with you and the others over small things that bothered me, and I beat you. I am truly sorry for that. It was then that Auntie Dorcas came and began to live with us. She kind of took over the role of mother, you know, and things have gotten better, don't you think? I have asked God to make me a better father, too."

"Yes, things are much better now, and I know you love me and the others," Benjamin agreed, "but why did she just leave us?"

"I guess she felt that this was no life for her and for her own children, so she is going to try working in the city and living on her own there."

"But that's wrong, isn't it?" Benjamin had obviously absorbed some teaching from him and through church.

"Yes, it is wrong for us to go against our promises, and marriage is a promise," began Jacob tenderly, "but sometimes people get so wrapped up in their own feelings, especially feelings of failure, that they do strange things to try to get out of the results of bad decisions they made before, or of bad situations they have been given by God. Perhaps

He was trying to teach her and me some lessons, and we have to try to figure out what those lessons are. Have you ever felt that God brought you into a bad situation, where you have to figure out what the lesson is, that you are supposed to learn from it?"

Now it was Benjamin's turn to be perplexed. "I guess when we had to flee Wuestenfelde, I wondered why God allowed the Catholic army to come to destroy it. Then, when Mother died as JJ was being born, I really wondered what God was up to."

"God doesn't always announce His plans for us 'way ahead of time, Benjamin. Sometimes He just lets things happen to us that challenge everything we think and are, and He wants us to trust him for the way to deal with the situation. He always provides a way for us, doesn't He?"

"He brought us to Altona, then he brought the Guenthers, next He used us when He brought the Roosens to us, then He brought Auntie Dorcas to us, so I guess He has always provided a way," the boy reasoned.

"God will continue to provide for us, Benjamin," Jacob continued. "Auntie Dorcas will stay with us, and she will be your mother from now on."

"Are you going to marry her?" Benjamin's curiosity couldn't let go.

"No, I can't marry her. Martina and I are still married, so I can't marry again." At this point, Dorcas called to say that Faspa was ready. This afternoon light meal was always a favorite of Benjamin's, so he led the way into the house. Jacob followed, wondering what was all going on in his son's mind. He was, after all, thirteen years old now, and questions of life and death were natural at his age.

Not many people could afford coffee, but Jacob had gotten some as payment for a cabinet he had built for a rich Jewish family. He and Dorcas enjoyed a cup together, as they watched the children eating their bread with homemade jam. For them, water was the drink offered, and they felt no sense of deprivation, for the water in Altona was good. Jacob mused on how his family had metamorphosed over the past months, as they had weathered one crisis after another. Dorcas contentedly watched over her 'family,' as they satisfied their late-afternoon hunger with satisfying bread and jam that she had made for them, and babbled about their activities and interests. Theirs had become a happy home once again, where they could mature in a healthy, loving atmosphere.

Jacob was asked to attend a meeting of the church deacons, and he went, not because he wanted to, but because he knew he had to. He had always enjoyed his meetings with the church council, but this time he dreaded going. The topic of discussion was known to him in his innermost thoughts, and that was what made him reluctant to go. What were the men going to say about his present family situation, now that Martina had left him? That was going to be gone into in great detail, as one after another questioned him about it.

He got to the meeting place after all the others had assembled, and greeted each of the well-known men personally, shaking hands all around and asking about personal matters as a matter of courtesy. It was only then that he noticed that Elder Janzen was in attendance. He greeted him warmly, for they had experienced many difficult situations together. Finally, he was bidden to take a seat in the circle of chairs around the table in the middle of the room. The Elder took the lead in addressing him.

"Jacob, we have heard that your marriage is in trouble. Would you please tell us what has happened?" he began.

"I don't want to give a wrong impression about anyone," Jacob started, "but I will give as much detail as required. I trust you will understand the entire situation, and not just make a judgment based on what you see openly, or on what others have told you, but on what you know to be the truth. As you all know, Rebekah died while delivering JJ, and Martina Roosen was our midwife. Because she had recently lost her husband in a work accident, she volunteered to continue to look after my children, which you also know, included the Guenthers' children, whom we took in when their parents died of the plague. She had two of her own, so that brought our new 'family' up to twelve children, made up of the children of three couples. We agreed that it would look bad for her to just move into my house to care for the children, but I had the little apartment off to the side, so I arranged for her to move into it. Without much thought, we agreed to marry, so that she could see her mother-role as being permanent. There was no particular love between us, but we thought we needed each other, and we based our marriage on that. She tried to look after all of the children while I went back to work, but this was simply not a skill she could master. Her interests were intellectual. She is a reader, a debater, and has an interest in learning about almost anything. Her children, too, are very smart. I was left with more and more of the housework and the disciplining of the children, while she bemoaned the fact that she was cooped up in a house all day with screaming children and had no outlet for her interests. I couldn't do anything about this, as I had to work to support the family. Fairly quickly we both slid deeper and deeper into depression, and things around the house just didn't get done at all. The children were being neglected, and we were simply not mentally or physically able to make decisions or to do anything about the problems that were all around us. I became violent with the children, beating them for very small things that irked me. You will remember that I withdrew from the deacons board at that time, as I simply didn't feel I had it in me to do God's work, when I simply couldn't do my own."

"In God's mercy, He sent my cousin, Dorcas, to us from Luebeck, where she had fled when we all left Wuestenfelde, and her experience as a Dorfschwester was soon put to good use in getting things under control in the household. A few days ago, Martina decided that she would leave. She got a job in Hamburg and moved back to her own home with her two children. Dorcas has stayed on to help me, and she has decided that this is going to be her life work, to raise my family for me. I have arranged that she lives in the apartment, so that she has space of her own. That is all I can tell you about my situation, gentlemen."

"Were you truly married to Martina?" Jonathan Dyck asked.

"You know we had a wedding ceremony, simple as it was, in my home – Elder Janzen can vouch for that – and before that, we were legally married at the Standesamt. I have the papers," Jacob replied.

"Was the marriage ever consummated?" Jonathan bored home mercilessly, showing where his true thoughts were directed.

"We tried to consummate the marriage, but neither of us was really in love with the other, so it was a pretty uneventful affair," Jacob replied, almost jokingly, but somewhat sheepishly. "After the first night, we didn't even attempt to get close."

"So, you would say you have a consummated marriage, which has dissolved," the deacon continued boring deeply.

"I would say we were legally married, and had the church's blessing on that, but it never amounted to a real marriage, in terms of love and attachment. As for consummation, Martina and I would both agree that it really never happened, though we tried," Jacob countered.

"Did you indicate to Martina that you wanted her to leave?" Jonathan seemed to be the one who had issues with his whole situation. Jacob recognized that his experience with his daughter's rape could have caused him to become so negative and yet so taken up with such moral details.

"I did not. She announced out of the blue that she was leaving, and having had her bags packed already, she left with her children. I have not seen her since."

"You know that, as head of a Christian household, you must keep your wife and children under your control, don't you? After all, you have been our preacher for many years." Jonathan still thought that everything could be solved with authority and force.

"I think that our Mennonite faith demands that we do not coerce other adults with any force at all, doesn't it?" Jacob replied defensively.

"In the family, force is demanded by God," the injured deacon replied. "As Paul says to Timothy, 'If a man know not how to rule his own house, how shall he take care of the church of God?' Paul also says that women are not to have knowledge on their own, but are to ask their husbands about things, as an act of subjection. In the henhouse, the rooster crows often to let the hens know who's the boss, and in the pasture, the bull bellows to let the cows know who's the boss."

Jacob looked pleadingly at the Elder, who nodded that he would speak to this. "In our Mennonite faith, we try to build our beliefs and our actions on what the Bible teaches us. In order to do this, we must apply the biblical concepts to our everyday lives. Sometimes these concepts are found in parts in several passages in the Bible, and are not simply a quotation from one verse. A person who is leading in the church must have his household under control, that is clear. What that means in individual cases is not so clear. We all interpret the Bible out of the background that we have come from, that shapes our thinking about whatever we see and hear. When a child disobeys its father, the father is commanded to use the rod, if necessary, to make the child obey. When an adult, in this case Jacob's wife, decides not to be in subjection to her husband, there is nowhere in the Bible that says he should beat her into submission. Paul also says what God had taught him, and left the results to God. I believe that is what Jacob has done in his case. One last question of you, Jacob: Do you intend to divorce Martina and to remarry?"

"No, I do not plan to do anything against Martina at all. She left voluntarily, and she can return voluntarily. I would not take her back into my house as a wife, but would allow her to live in the apartment. Dorcas plans to stay, and that is a good arrangement for my children, so it is good for me, as well. I would have to take Dorcas into the house then, but we could crowd the children together more as we did before when she first came and make that possible."

"Then I believe we should simply leave the situation as it is. Jacob cannot do anything more about it, without divorcing Martina, and he has come up with what I believe is a good biblical solution to the problem," the Elder concluded.

The deacons, with one exception, murmured their acceptance of what their Elder had stated. Jonathan became quite angry and stomped out of the meeting, slamming the door loudly behind him. In this way, he was 'voicing' his strong objection to the lack of strong discipline that he had hoped would have been placed on the offending Jacob. The Elder continued, somewhat quietly, "Our brother obviously does not agree with our interpretation of the scriptures. Let us leave him to sort out his views and try to conclude this case. We must decide what is going to happen to Jacob, insofar as his role as a preacher in the Mennonite Church is concerned."

Jacob took the matter into his own hands, "I believe that, for my own personal good and my family's, such as it now is, that I should no longer be the preacher in the Altona congregation. I already declined to preach during my time of depression, and I also resigned my position as a council member. It would not be fair to my children, if I tried to continue to lead the congregation, with all that this demands, and also to try to bring in enough income to support their needs. We can manage well, with Cousin Dorcas at the helm in our household, and I can get my mental health back, so that I can be of as much help to the community as possible."

That statement took the wind out of the deacons' sails, and they sat there like becalmed boats on the North Sea. No one spoke. No one offered any alternatives.

"Who will then speak in your services?" the Elder broke the silence.

"I guess we can take turns," the deacon at the far end of the table ventured. He had not spoken during the meeting.

"What about Jonathan? He didn't seem very happy with the way we'd handled this matter," Jacob Wiens asked tentatively.

"We can ask him if he would like to be included in the list, and if not, then we just go on from there," David Froese thought. "At our next meeting of the church, we can decide whether he should continue to be a deacon."

That seemed to settle the matter to everyone's satisfaction. The Elder closed the meeting with a passionate prayer for the Altona church, and for Jacob and his family situation. He also included the men who were about to take on more active preaching roles. In conclusion, he lifted up Jonathan Dyck and his distressed family, and asked that he be given the Spirit's insight. The men gathered around Jacob after the meeting had been adjourned, and asked whether there was anything they could do to help him and his family. A few ideas were brought out that might help in this. Then, all went to their homes.

Chapter 10

Life settled into a routine in the Altona congregation and also in the Derksen household. Dorcas's management skills and personal ability to deal with daily situations proved to be the tonic that brought new life to the beleaguered family. Her humor and candor were appreciated by everyone. She became the new mother-figure in Jacob Derksen's household, and everyone loved her. Jacob's recovery from the stress-related breakdown, however, took some time. Dorcas prepared warm poultices for his neck in the evenings, tenderly massaging his tightened muscles and applying healing balms to his aches and pains with consummate skill. She prepared his favorite dishes for supper. She roasted the bag of cherry pits in the oven before sending him off to bed with this wonderful warming pillow. Bit by bit, his energy returned, and with it, his humor and intellectual capabilities. He became more and more the real father to his children and the Guenthers' and instructed them in the things that were important to their future roles. He occasionally lapsed back into depression, but the lapses were shorter and shorter, until there didn't seem to be any signs of that malady from day to day. It seemed that these occurred when thoughts of Rebekah returned to him, but he did not want to forget her. It was part of his mourning process, he reckoned. Then, his attitude would change to one of positive wholesomeness, and he was back to his former self. Life seemed almost too good to be true.

"I left a book here," the words came loudly from the front door, just as the family was sitting down to the evening meal. Everyone looked toward the door, as Martina walked in. She assumed that this was still her house, to enter and leave at will without formalities.

"Uh, which book are you talking about," Dorcas took charge.

"Jacob knows, it's the one in the bureau drawer in our room," Martina replied impertinently.

"You took all your things from the bureau drawers, Martina," Jacob replied evenly.

"I want to see for myself," demanded Martina, haughtily.

"Go ahead, there is only the girls' stuff in the drawers, that I know of," said Jacob in resignation. Martina immediately went to their former bedroom to check, but found that Jacob was no longer using that room, which had been given to the girls, because it was the largest one. The bureau had been left there, however, so Martina searched through their things for the missing book. Not finding it, she began searching through other places and other rooms. Still not finding it, she came back in exasperation.

"You've thrown it away. You destroyed my book," she yelled.

"Nothing of yours has been destroyed, and nothing was left to hide. You have nothing in this house. Martina, I did not send you away; you left because you wanted to, so please don't come back and accuse me of doing things to you. I've never done anything to you, and when you are ready, you may return to live in the apartment," Jacob stated, with some emphasis now. This was news to Dorcas, who was living in the apartment, so she raised her eyebrows at the suggestion that she might have to share it with Martina, or move out into the main part of the house.

Martina stood there in mock rage, for there had been no book. She simply wanted to see how Jacob was managing without her. She had seen that everything was in the best of order, and there seemed to be tranquility in the house.

Jacob continued, though all the children could hear the whole conversation, "Martina, you must learn some things, and you cannot probably learn them without having your own will engaged. You have done that, and you have decided to move out with your children, who I took on as my own. I don't know what it is that you need to learn, but I trust that you will find it in your new life. In the meantime, please allow me and my family to go on with our lives."

Martina shot a glaring look at him, whirled on her heel and left the house in her rage, which by now was becoming quite real.

The house became very still, the by now cold meal lying flatly on the plates. Dorcas glanced over at Jacob, who maintained his inscrutable gaze on his plate.

"Daddy, why did Mommy Martina come in and talk like that? Why did she go through all my things?" Elizabeth's plaintive questions brought her father to the reality of the moment.

"Your Mommy thought she had left a book here, and she wanted to find it," Dorcas answered for him.

"She's not my real Mommy; you're my real Mommy," the girl responded.

"Well, I guess you could say that I am now," Dorcas laughed. That brought some serenity to the room, and Dorcas offered to warm up their cold supper plates. They all volunteered to eat it the way it was; indeed, Benjamin and Joshua had already wolfed down most of theirs.

For some weeks nothing of importance happened. The children went back to school, except for Agnes, Willy and JJ, who remained at home with Dorcas. She relished the extra time this gave her to teach them things appropriate for their ages. Jacob was content with his work at the wagon factory. All seemed to be going well.

News came through that a peace settlement had been made in Luebeck between the Danes and the imperial army in May, and that the war in their area was done. There had still been fighting, but it had now shifted to being between Swedes and Poles, but even that had been settled at the Peace of Altmark. The imperial troops had moved south, where the French were now engaging them in skirmishes. The Mennonite leaders thought that this would bring a new era of prosperity and freedom to them, and they were discussing plans for expansion of the various businesses that their enterprising ways had initiated in the last two and one-half years, since they had fled Wuestenfelde.

Then, a visit from the mayor of Altona brought them up short. George Toews, the Schultze of the Mennonite community came to the other leaders and announced what he had been told. They faced a new series of taxes that would cripple them in their endeavors, and they were required to hold their services quietly, without singing or instruments. Apparently the Lutheran merchants and factory owners, who made up the majority of the town's populace, were envious of the success of the Mennonites and the Jews, so they looked for ways to bite hard into their profits, making their continued existence in the town very insecure. That was exactly what the townspeople wanted. Although they had tolerated the Mennonites, they showed their true colors by limiting their activities to the point of throttling them.

Jacob began to take stock in the wagon factory, and he realized that he could not compete with the larger businesses in Hamburg. Sales would drop to zero very quickly, once the present orders were filled. Then, one by one, he received letters of cancellation of the existing orders, leaving him with a number of completed wagons in stock, with no sales in sight.

Business in the brewery was going well, and the Mennonites had been able to meet their obligations to pay for recruitment of troops for the Danish king, but now that the war was essentially over, the Mennonite leaders assumed that they could stop paying the tax. That proved to be a wrong assumption. Once a tax is instituted, it generally remains in effect, even if the situation changes. That left them with essentially no profits at all, and considerable inventory that had been paid in advance. The leaders took stock and accounted for every piece of equipment, At this point Jacob, who was no longer on the community council, went to George Toews and suggested that the time had come for drastic action. He thought the community should migrate to West Prussia, where many of their Mennonite relatives and friends were living quite peaceably. George did not think that many would want to go, but he would bring it to the council. He even suggested that Jacob come to the meeting himself to bring his suggestion before the men in person.

Jacob went home to discuss the prospects with Dorcas. She was not surprised, knowing a bit of the jealousy that existed among Lutherans against the Mennonites. The idea of moving again did not appeal to her in the slightest, but she agreed that it was probably the only thing they could do. Some Mennonites would be able to remain in Altona and Hamburg, she thought, and ply their trade quite quietly, but the majority would have to go, so as to make the impression that the Lutherans had won the day for their artisans and sales.

The meeting with the community leaders was amicable and short. Jacob presented his case well, and several of the men agreed that it might be best to move to Royal Prussia. Reports from there through their Elder had been quite positive. The Polish nobles near Danzig were actually asking for Mennonites with their Lowlands background to come and help drain the Vistula Delta swamps and make them fit for agriculture. The continued contagions of malaria were also of great concern to the people in the region, and draining the swamps would take away the breeding grounds of the pesky mosquitoes that carried what they termed swamp fever. Tradesmen were also needed, and these might be able to find work in the city. There were also restrictions on the activities of the Mennonites, but they were not as obnoxious to them as they were where they were now. A meeting was scheduled for after church the following Sunday, when Jacob could present this proposal to the entire group. He could have people contact him to see who wanted to go, and then he could organize the expedition.

Sunday dawned clear and cool. Autumn winds were blowing, making the sun's rays seemingly dissolve before they touched the skin. Word had gotten around that there was to be an important announcement, so everyone tried to get there for the service. That caused some problems, as there weren't enough benches to go around. The younger men made way for women, children and older men, standing at the sides and back of the wagon factory, or perched on favorite beams above the crowd. The normal men-on-one-side women-on-the-other-side order seemed quite naturally to dissolve in the crowded quarters. The service was not auspicious, with one of the less eloquent deacons delivering a belabored message from an obscure passage. Since he was speaking in Dutch, which was not his main language any more, and most of the rest of their dealings in the homes were done in the local dialect, younger ones, in particular, had difficulty following what the man was trying to say at all, let alone understand the spiritual implications of the message. Everyone, including the speaker, was relieved when he was finished. Another deacon closed the meeting in prayer, and Jacob was called upon to make his announcement.

"My dear brothers and sisters in Christ, I would like to make a proposal today," he began.

"You should try making one to your wife," Jonathan Dyck called out loudly.

Jacob took no notice of the man's remark. "We know that the war in this area is probably over, because peace treaties have been signed between imperial troops and the Danes. We hear that the same has occurred between the Swedes and the Poles. That leaves the whole north coast of the Baltic Sea open for travel and for settling. Many of our brothers and sisters have gone to Royal Prussia, and a few have even gone as far as East Prussia, seeking security and peace for their families and for our dearly held beliefs. We thought that, with the war being ended, we could now give ourselves more fully to our work, and that we could make a good profit from it, to help our needy families, but our Count will not hear of our stopping to pay the recruitment tax, which is killing us financially. With that over our heads, we can't hope to enlarge our factory or our brewery, nor can we expand our textile shipments, so we have very little room to maneuver in our dealings with Altona or Hamburg. That seems to me to leave us only the option of moving once again, this time further east, to Royal Prussia. The leaders in Danzig and the Vistula Delta area are inviting us to come and help them drain their swamps and establish healthy farms in the area, as well as to use our occupational skills in the city, to aid their manufacturing industry. Anyone who is interested in coming along, please see me during the next week, and I will begin organizing the expedition to Royal Prussia."

There were many murmurs throughout the building, as people got up to return to their homes. Their time in Altona had not been all that long, but they felt somewhat at home there, so a decision to leave would be difficult to make. Some showed obvious scorn for the idea, while others seemed to take it almost humorously, but many showed obvious interest.

It was then that Jacob saw her. Martina had come to the meeting, and she had heard everything he had said. She came toward him, this time without the scornful demeanor of the previous times, but with what seemed almost a repentant spirit, he thought. Jacob waited where he was, just in front of the pulpit, and she proceeded to come through the crowd to him. Dorcas was still seated on a bench, with a group of ladies around her, and was totally unaware of what was transpiring elsewhere in the building.

"I want to talk with you, Jacob," Martina began, then sobs came throbbing from her throat.

Jacob put his arm around her large frame and sought to comfort her. He led her to the front bench and bade her sit down. He found his clean handkerchief and offered it to her. She nodded her thanks and wiped her eyes, then blew her nose loudly, wrapped up the cloth and put it into her ample bosom.

"I am making it on my own in Hamburg, Jacob, but I can't stop thinking about my relationship with you and with the church here in Altona. I didn't know that you were making an announcement this morning, but

I'm glad I heard it," she began. "I am sorry for the way I ran out on you, but I don't think that our marriage would have worked out anyway. We are too different to get along well, and I have no domestic skills to offer you and the children. They are far better off without me, and Dorcas is doing a wonderful job with them, I could see when I visited you. I had no book to look for; I just wanted to get one more glimpse into your life, to see that everything would be alright. I don't know whether the church will take me back, but I want to come back. I won't even offer to come back to you. As I said, I don't really believe it would work out anyway, so I think I'll just remain in Hamburg and come out for church services here, if the deacons will let me. If you are gone to Prussia, then our relationship will be over, even though we won't be divorced, and we can begin a new life apart from each other and forget each other."

"What about Gerritt and Lizzy?" Jacob asked tenderly.

"Gerritt and Lizzy are both in Latin school, doing very well. Gerritt has joined a small company in the cloth business and has convinced them that there is a market for stockings, so hosiery is now part of our daily conversation. He continues to excel in his subjects, and of all things, he is talking about becoming a Mennonite preacher."

"Are you sure you don't want to return to my house? My offer was genuine; you could have the apartment free of rent, if you wish. I'm not sure what we would do with your children, but somehow we should be able to make it work out for you," Jacob offered.

"No, Jacob, I think it is best if we just separate and go our own ways, then your children will not be encumbered with my presence, and you can get on with your life. We never had a marriage anyway. Perhaps we should ask for an annulment. The City of Altona Standesamt would likely give it to us without too much of a problem, if we went in together and applied."

That was an idea Jacob had not ever considered, but it made sense. They had not really consummated the marriage, as the law or the church understood it, and then both of them would be unencumbered. They agreed on a date to go to the Standesamt, to see whether it was possible to arrange an annulment. She then left.

Dorcas, in the meantime, had finished her conversation with the other ladies, and looking for Jacob, saw him and Martina talking amicably. She wondered what had gone on between them, but she held her peace, just indicating that she was ready to leave for home. Jacob bowed, offered her his arm and escorted her out of the building to their horse and carriage.

"We are going to annul our wedding," Jacob said out of the blue, as they were driving home. "Martina and I agreed that our marriage had never really been a marriage anyway, so we are going to the Standesamt to get the marriage annulled."

Now it was Dorcas's turn to be stunned. "What brought Martina to our meeting, anyway?" she asked.

"She had a change of heart and wanted to apologize for her behavior at our house the other day and to come back to the Mennonite church here, so she happened to be there for our meeting. She expressed her regrets for leaving us, but she felt that our marriage would never work, so it would be best to annul it, and get that monkey off our backs."

"That seems like a good idea, but what about the church? Will they accept an annulment of the marriage and reinstate you as preacher?" she queried.

"It doesn't matter to me. I really don't need to be the preacher. Besides, if I take a group to Prussia, I won't be here to preach anyway."

"That is true, but what about when we get there, will you, if you are the leader of the group, also be expected to be the preacher?"

"The people will have to decide that. If they ask me, I could consider it. I enjoyed preaching. But, remember, I also stopped being a community councilor, because of my condition. I am now taking on a much greater role than that, and preaching would double the pressure on all of us."

"I think you're ready for it," she replied with a smile, putting her hand on his shoulder. "You're my hero-cousin, and I believe in you."

"I'm glad someone believes in me. And by the way, you said, 'when *we* get there' to Prussia, so I welcome you to the group as my first applicant." He took the reins in one hand and squeezed her arm playfully.

Chapter 11

Annulment proceedings dragged on mercilessly. There were mountains of forms to fill out. The embarrassments of the questions Jacob and Martina had to answer about the state of their relationship left both of them deflated, and Jacob neared going into a depression again. Still, they persisted, and finally, the papers were received that they had never really consummated their marriage, and that therefore, the marriage was annulled according to law.

Martina seemed to disappear into Hamburg with her children. Jacob, on the other hand, was busy in Altona, trying to begin the organization of the trek to West Prussia. He made a trip there to see for himself what the prospects would be. He met with leaders of the Mennonite communities in Danzig and in the delta region, to see where it would be best to settle the group. The need was for settlers to drain the swamps and clear them, so that malaria would no longer infest the area, and so that this rich land could be made productive. Polish Catholic princes that ruled the outlying areas were especially interested in bringing in Mennonites, for they had seen how industrious they were, and they knew that their origins in the Low Countries had prepared them for the task they hoped would bring them better health and prosperity.

Merchants in Danzig were not as excited about having competition arriving from the West, but they agreed that there was room for a limited number of them around Danzig, and there certainly was room for those who could produce food for sale. Eventually it was agreed that the main settlement would be northwest of Marienburg. Because of the extensive areas of deep swamp grass that grew there as cheap hay, which could also serve as material for constructing temporary houses, Jacob decided that he would name the settlement Heubuden, which meant Hay Booths. Jacob was reminded of the Old Testament Feast of Tabernacles, when the Israelites commemorated their deliverance from Egypt and their trek through the desert, that they had lived in temporary shelters made up of whatever materials they could find. They would have to work quickly in order to escape the attacks by the mosquitoes. Perhaps, if they came early enough in the season, they could drain the swamps and prevent the pesky creatures from multiplying, by taking away their breeding grounds. That would also give them time to break up the soil, dry it out enough, and plant a crop and some gardens. There would be a lot of work, but the local Mennonites, and even the Catholics around them were willing to lend a hand and equipment.

Fall work in Altona consisted mainly of harvesting crops and gardens, and preserving what had been gathered, to provide for the winter that was surely coming. The men were mainly involved in the harvesting, and the women in the preserving and storing. Children were commandeered to help; this was for their benefit, as well. School shut down for a couple of weeks in fall to provide all the families time to finish the work before them, without the stress of also having to get their children ready for school. The problem for the teachers of having a few children there and many missing was thus avoided, making most people in the community happy. The teachers also volunteered their help in the harvesting. Artisans who worked mainly in town continued to do so, but every hand that could be made available was put to work.

Because there would be no sales, and thus there was no need for production, the wagon factory workers were given time to help with the harvest, too. Cloth merchants helped when they were in town, which was only a day or two for each of them. The brewery kept producing, as it provided the money to pay the recruitment tax demanded by the Count. The barley that was harvested was deposited in the brewery's bins, to be malted throughout the coming year and brewed into their by now famous beer. Community spirit was at its highest during harvest season, when every available man or woman worked together for the common good.

Crews of men and able-bodied women were sent out to the outlying fields to harvest grain, whether wheat, barley, rye, or oats. Each had its particular purpose in the nourishment of either mankind or beast.

The sickle was the tool of the harvest. Like a curved scimitar, it was used to cut the stalks of grain at just above ankle height. The stalks of ripe grain were gathered in the other hand until there were sufficient to bind into a sheaf. This was done by twisting a few strands of stalk together to make a sort of rope, which was then wrapped around the sheaf and pushed under itself by the men and women doing the harvesting. These sheaves were then gathered together into fours or sixes and stacked one against the other as shocks. After drying in the warm breeze for a couple of days, these were then picked up by horse-drawn wagons and brought to the hard surface where they would be threshed. In the two years since they had arrived, the Mennonites had been able to secure adequate storage facilities for the grain, which could then be distributed to the families throughout the winter for reasonable payments.

Garden produce was also harvested. Beans, which by now included haricot and pole-climbing varieties brought in from the Americas by returning explorers and multiplied by seed growers and horticulturalists in many European countries, were dried and kept in cool storage, as peas had been for many generations. These now formed the staple of their diet, along with grain products. Potatoes, also from the New World and by now also grown widely in northern Europe, were dug out, and then having had the dirt knocked off them, were dried and taken to root cellars along with other root vegetables like carrots, beets, parsnips and horse radish, covered in dried walnut leaves. Cabbage heads could be stored in frost-free dry storage places for a number of months, so some firm heads were put on shelves in the root cellars, while the majority of heads were simply shredded and put into crocks with salt water covering the cabbage, to produce sauerkraut. Fruit was harvested, cut into small pieces and dried in the warm fall sunshine, or put on wire racks with warm air circulating through them, to dry. The various varieties, which included apples, cherries, pears, plums and quinces, were then stored in earthenware jars with lids, ready to enhance many a creative recipe. First cherries, then plums, had already been so prepared during the months before, as they ripened. Berries, such as raspberries and strawberries, called earth berries by these folks, had also been dried for future use. Many had found their way, along with cherries and plums, into Moos, which the Mennonites had begun very early to enjoy, and which recipes followed them wherever they moved. Dried fruits from southern Europe, which included peaches, apricots, raisins and currants, were not generally available, except to the rich merchants of cities like Hamburg and to nobles, such as Counts von Schauenburg.

Dorcas fitted right into all of these activities, having grown up with them in Wuestenfelde, and she provided light-hearted conversation among the women, as she worked shoulder-to-shoulder with them, shelling peas or beans, or supervising the older children as they cut fruit and got it ready for drying.

Once the harvest was in and the gardens cleared and stored, the men set about preparing for the butchering, which came next. Each family brought their pig or pigs, and a few steers were also brought to a central place, which was where they also met to worship, and which had served as their wagon factory. Large tables were constructed, where the meat would be cut up into the various pieces that would be used for specific meals – hams and bacon, mainly. All the rest was cut into small pieces and fed into the hand-operated meat grinder. Large kettles with fire boxes underneath and stove pipes sticking out the back, called Mia-Grope, were heated, and the fatty pieces, now ground fine, were put into them for rendering. Older children were put to stirring the slippery mass of fat with large wooden paddles, to keep it from sticking on the bottom, before melting down into clear lard. Men continued to cut meat and fat chunks, while some ground them fine for further production, the fat going into the pots, and the meaty portions going into piles to be made into sausage.

Meanwhile, in a clean area of the shop, the women sat around large tubs with paring knives and water basins, cleaning the intestines so that they could be used as casings for the sausages. The stomach was cleaned for <u>Leberwurst</u>, which was made from scraps of meat and the pork liver. A basin of blood had been kept for making <u>Blutwurst</u>. Even the bladders were cleaned and used, either for sausage casings, or for making flotation devices or small bellows that could be used elsewhere. It seemed that every part of the animal was utilized somehow. One jokingly said that every part of the pig was used except the "oink." The spareribs were put into the rendered lard to be deep-fried, and this was the only fresh meat that was generally eaten on the day of the pig killing. Some of the women were busy roasting chickens and making Pluma Moos, dishes traditionally eaten on butchering days.

The steers that were slaughtered were treated similarly, but the heart, liver and tongue were kept for special feasting. Someone even volunteered to take the kidneys, and another took the stomach home to clean up for tripe. Tallow was kept for making candles, and a bit of the beef was usually added to the pork sausage, as well. Otherwise, the beef was cut into thin strips and dried or smoked, which were the only effective ways of preservation at that time. A later butchering day would be arranged during the cold weather, so that the meat could be frozen in larger chunks. These were bundled and put into cellars with large blocks of ice, where they were kept frozen until spring.

The hams were laid in brine for six to eight weeks. The meat from around the pig's head, as well as the knuckles, hocks and feet were cleaned and cooked along with some pieces of skin to provide gelatin, in which they were then embedded, to form head cheese.

A small chamber was sealed off and a rack was lowered from the top, so that the sausages could be draped over the rods. When it was full, a fire was started on the ground underneath, and pieces of selected wood were placed on it, to provide just the right flavor in the smoking process. Smoking provided three basic components: smoked meat has a delightful flavor, it keeps at room temperature much longer than fresh meat, and it helps keep the flies from laying their eggs in the meat. Sausages needed a warm fast fire with plenty of smoke immediately, so a different wood was used for that, along with oat straw to provide a hot steamy smoke, and then they were finished and taken down. Bacon slabs were then hung on the racks, and a slow fire with beech and willow wood was started under them, which was kept up for several days, to give just the right flavor and preservation. The finished slabs were then seen hanging in every kitchen, above the stove, where the women could cut strips off to add to their dishes.

Weeks later, the hams would also be smoked, after they had cured in the salt and honey brine, usually with beech wood. The combined effects of the brine and the smoking kept them through the winter and well into spring. The un-smoked beef was usually dried, so that it could be used sparingly throughout the winter, but pork did not respond as well to drying, so it was generally put in brine and/or smoked.

This life rhythm had been forged among the Mennonites during the previous century of settlement, in Friesland and Flanders, in Wuestenfelde and in Prussia, as well as in Altona. There was regular contact between all of them, both through the elders, who traveled widely, and through the cloth merchants, who also visited broadly. Jacob was especially concerned that enough was prepared in advance, so that his growing group would be well provided for, both during their trek and afterwards, as they settled in Heubuden. Various families had decided that their future lay, not in the confines of the town of Altona, but in the swamps of Royal Prussia, and were signing up with Jacob to make the trek, come springtime. Optimism was growing that they would be freer to practice their faith than they presently were under the dominance of a major European trading city, and that they would be able to forge a new and prosperous life for themselves under different circumstances.

Chapter 14

Gerritt Roosen needed to speak to Jacob. Something was pressing upon him, and he needed fatherly counsel. He showed up one day with no warning to seek Jacob out. Finding him in the wagon factory, looking at a piece of equipment that needed to be dismantled for transport to their new colony, he asked if he could speak with him privately.

"Come over here with me. There are a few tree stumps cut off just right for us to sit on. My, you have grown into a fine young man, Gerritt. You must be about eighteen now, I believe?" Jacob wanted the nervous fellow to be calm in his presence.

"Yes, I have finished Latin school, and I am working full-time with the clothing producers. I have introduced stocking-making into our offerings, and business seems to be going well. The merchants say they can't get enough of them, and our people are forced to work very hard, just to keep up with the most urgent demands. I am planning to increase the size of my operation and to hire more stocking makers, to meet the demands in the Hanseatic cities along the coast. The war is still hampering our getting into some ports, but most are open to shipping, and we are doing a very good business." *The boy is eloquent, but then he has always been intelligent,* Jacob thought, *and he has a resonant* tenor voice, which is an interesting mixture of his father's baritone and his mother's nasal wheezing.

"How are your mother and your sister?" Jacob could not help but inquire, for he somehow felt a bit responsible for the woman and her family.

"Mother still has her job in the bookstore, so that brings in enough to keep her. I can help out now with family expenses, so we have moved into a better house. She would like to attend church more, but she is very tired, after working all day and studying all evening. Lizzy is finishing school this year, and she wants to go on to university to become a doctor," Gerritt offered. "Here is our new address," he handed Jacob a piece of paper with something written on it.

"You say your mother is studying?" Jacob was not surprised, but his curiosity was roused.

"Yes, she found a professor at the university who has taken her on as a private student. She is reading much in philosophy and history now, and writing many papers," the young man replied. "But, that is not why I came. I want to know what I would need to do to become a Mennonite minister."

"A Mennonite minister? Why would you, a successful businessman at the tender age of eighteen, be interested in the ministry, especially in a Mennonite church, where we don't pay our preachers?" Jacob was now really surprised.

"I believe God has opened the way for me to be successful in business, and I feel I can offer Him myself to preach in the Mennonite church. I do believe in the truth of what we hear preached, and I believe God has given me a mind to study the truth and pass it on to many people. The younger generation would like to hear it from one of their own, I believe, so I will have their ear, perhaps even more than their present preacher has," there was a twinkle in Gerritt's eyes at that last statement, which was meant as a good-natured jibe at Jacob.

"I am no longer preacher in the Mennonite church, Gerritt, though I appreciate your good natured statement. My health condition has not allowed me to take on such an added stressful job now, but I could talk with the deacons and with the elder, and we will see what can be done. In the meantime, let's go over to the house, and I will give you a couple of books from Menno Simon to read, and you can begin to prepare yourself for being a Mennonite preacher."

The young man proved to be an able student, and he was quickly brought before the council of deacons for an interview, previous to his being allowed to preach his first sermon. He would be coached by Jacob, who took a fatherly interest in the developing young man. The sermon was, as he predicted, especially heard by the young people in the congregation, but even the older ones commented on his depth of perception and his knowledge of the Scriptures. The deacons readily made way for him to preach oftener, and all seemed to be happy about the new star that had popped up above their horizon. Jacob continued to share his small library of Menno's writings with his protégé, and to coach him in his preparation of messages.

An amazing thing began to happen in the church. Jonathan Dyck and his wife and daughter were seen in the services on an ever more regular basis, listening intently to the messages of the young prodigy. Then one day, after the service, Gerritt could be seen moving in the direction of Suzie. He caught her eye and motioned that he would like to talk with her. She showed her abject panic, but allowed him to come nearer. He motioned that she should come away from the others, so she looked at her father questioningly. He was taken up with another discussion and didn't notice his daughter, so she allowed herself to move carefully in Gerritt's direction. As they got a bit away from the others, Gerritt simply said to her, "Suzie, I think I want to get to know you better. You are a very pretty young woman, and I think you would be someone I could enjoy spending some time with. Do you mind, if I take an interest in you?"

"You know what happened to me," began the frightened girl, and faltered.

"But you couldn't help that, and God hasn't left you. I think we could learn to be good friends, and who knows, we might even get interested in each other," Gerritt said disarmingly.

"I think you are a wonderful preacher, and I guess you might be a good person to get to know. I haven't spoken to many people since what happened that first night in Altona, so I will need a lot of practice, before I can speak as well as you can," she began to open up to the affable young man before her.

"Let's not hurry," Gerritt suggested, "We are both still pretty young, but I wanted you to know that your situation can be healed by having someone that trusts you, and by someone that cares for you in spite of all that has happened to you."

"Oh, thank you," she blushed, and went over to her parents, who were looking quizzically her way.

As winter came, and work seemed to have frozen to the ground, Jacob prepared for another trip to West Prussia. He was going to secure written permission from the authorities for their settling in Heubuden, and for them to work in the various trades that were represented in the group, as well as to begin the draining of the swamps to open them up for agriculture. He also wanted to find out what kinds of agriculture were most successful, and what types of plants would flourish in the soggy soil of the marshes, even though they were drained. He had talked with some experts from Friesland, who told him what to watch for in such a venture, and what types of things they had found to grow successfully during the first years of swamp reclamation, so he was going with information in hand, to compare with local ideas and practice. As accompaniment, he decided to ask Gerritt and Benjamin to come with him. They would be a great help in carrying bags, and they would also learn about this other part of Europe, where so many Mennonites had found refuge for a difficult century. Together, they began to make preparations to take a horse and carriage, which was also equipped with sled runners that could be lowered, in case the snow got too deep for wheels to traverse. This was a very handy vehicle, made for the two main road conditions that this region offered – passable and bad.

The boys accepted their roles with relish, making plans alongside Jacob for adventures of their own. Jacob enjoyed the camaraderie that had developed between them, though there were over three years' difference in their ages. Benjamin seemed to thrive in having a big brother figure to look up to and to emulate, and Gerritt had an easy grace about him, that made him a natural leader. Gerritt had Martina bring him books on the area they would be seeing, so that he could prepare himself for what might occur. He brought them along when he came over to Derksens, and together, he and Benjamin, along with a tribe of eager young onlookers, would pore over the information the books brought into their lives. They were also dreaming of the great trek that would take them along those same roads to their new home next spring.

The trip was begun on a cold snowy January day. The horses quickly became coated with hoarfrost, as they stood patiently waiting for the carriage to be loaded. Finally, they were ready, and with many hugs and tears, the men left down the street that connected to the road toward West Prussia. At first it went right through the heart of Hamburg, and there Martina stood at the side of the street, waving to her son and her former 'acting' husband and his son. They waved back in return, and the horses were now anxious to get moving a bit more quickly, so that they broke into a trot, setting up a regular jingling of harness and wheels. Soon the big city was behind them, as they headed toward Luebeck. The shaded roads, where in summertime the branches from each side would meet over their heads, were now laced with hoarfrost, making them appear like a lace border around a pastoral painting.

They took the coastal road that would take them through the Hanseatic cities of Rostock and Stralsund, before reaching Danzig. The Treaty of Luebeck, concluded in May of 1629 had taken the Danes out of the war, and the Peace of Altmark, negotiated in September of 1629 had made peace between the Swedes and the Poles. No army ventured into war in the cold of winter, Jacob mused, so there would be no military activity for them to have to skirt on their trip. It was good that Jacob did not know that Sweden was at that very moment scheming how they could become more involved in the German duchy of Brandenburg, once spring had come. Jacob thought that, based on what he had seen of armies, they would probably not become active until May, which would give him time to make his trek with the Mennonite families, if they went in April. They should be able to arrive with their material possessions relatively intact, he thought, if they were careful, and if bandits did not bother them.

The boys, on the other hand, were captivated by the destruction they witnessed all along the road. The troops had left a desolate land, denuded of vegetation and robbed of its villages. Soldiers had taken whatever they wanted and had destroyed the rest wherever they went. At first it was almost like a game to them, but as they saw more and more of it, the scope of the damage was just too great to be a game anymore. War was not pretty, they saw, and it did not leave a trail of beauty in its wake. Ideology was literally wasted on the landscape and the people, and most of the damage was hidden by the covering of snow. Everywhere there were camps of refugees from the war, begging beside the road for something to eat and something warm to wear. The boys became very sober and silent, the more they saw of such atrocities.

Jacob drove his horse carefully, for he could not afford to stop at an inn and trade horses, as the post coaches did. They stopped for the night in secluded inns a bit off the main road, so as not to draw attention to themselves and the things they had with them. It was Jacob's firm belief that God was looking after them and protecting them from the harm lurking around every bend in the road. Whether he was right in so assuming or not, they seemed to be divinely protected, for nothing untoward happened along the way, other than that some of their clothing found its way onto an especially poorly dressed and very cold beggar.

The journey took over a week, for they could not make quick progress in the cold weather on uncleared roads. By this time the boys were getting quite impatient, but Jacob remained cheerful, and he found ways to interest them in things along the way, distracting them from their impatience. One such effort was to allow the boys to alternate driving the horse.

Finally, they were getting close to Danzig, and Jacob consulted his papers at their last visit to an inn before the city, to find the address of the people with whom they were going to stay. He found that this was to be in Marienburg, another day's travel beyond the city. Finding a way around the edge of Danzig, he headed the carriage toward the smaller city. Villages carried either German or Polish names, depending on the nationality of their settlers and their princes. The horse was getting tired, and they had not been able to stop for long periods to feed it; rather, its feeding time came late in the day, after they had checked into a local inn. That resulted in its getting thinner, for they were constantly moving. Jacob was thankful that its shoes had not come loose along the way, possibly injuring its hooves. That would have meant a long delay. As they got to Marienburg, they found the house where they were to stay, and found that their Mennonite colleagues had plenty of hay and oats for the horse, and there was a blacksmith in the town that could check the horse's hooves, trimming and tightening as necessary.

The Mennonite groups in the area were scattered in various towns and villages throughout the delta. Although there was fairly regular contact between them, their activities were somewhat independent of one another. Anton Thiessen, their host, was Schultze of the group in Marienburg, and he had a good grasp of the situation among the various groups. He could also advise on possibilities in the proposed new settlement of Heubuden, which Jacob intended to begin in spring. Together, the men and boys visited the site that would be where the village was to be situated, and sought to discover where it would be best to dig a well. This would be the first need for their new community. The water table was almost at ground level, so it should not be difficult to find a suitable site, they reckoned. The water was not the best tasting as a result of runoff mixing with the ground water, but it would have to do. Perhaps they would have to strain it before drinking, to remove whatever soil and insects were lurking in it. Knowledge of germs had not yet reached them, so only the physical properties that could be seen, smelled or tasted were considered as important.

Even in winter the landscape showed that there were swamps in every direction. Since there was nowhere for the water to drain, they would have to devise a way to pump it away. That would mean the need for a windmill, an apparatus that was quite common in the Low Countries. The swampy lowlands in the Old Country had been cleared for several hundred years now, and were now productive farmlands, so Jacob thought this area, too, could be reconstructed to become useful to their group. The <u>Werder</u> on which they were standing, somewhat higher than the swamps around them, would be an ideal location for the village. Other villages in the area surrounding them had also built on these slightly raised areas, to provide protection from the inevitable spring flooding that inundated the lowlands around them. In the Low Countries, <u>Werders</u> were often constructed by bringing in dirt from where a pond was designated to be, before the village was built upon them. There they were called <u>Wierds</u>.

Jacob talked long into the night with Anton, seeking to find out what would be available to his group, when they arrived, and what they might have to bring with them. As he talked with the seasoned settler, he realized that their wagons would be very full, and that they would have to seek a number of additional wagons and teams, in order to bring all their needed goods along. Some heavier wagons with wider wheels would have to be fabricated, and four-horse teams sought, in order to bring the heavier items. Jacob dutifully took notes on everything as they talked, so as not to forget anything of importance, once he was back with the group in Altona. Anton took note of several things, too, that he would have to organize beforehand, in order to make their settling in as painless as possible. Perhaps he could get his men started on digging the well as soon as the frost left, but that would depend on what preparations had to be made for spring seeding, and how quickly they were able to get onto the land after the annual flood waters receded.

After a week with the Thiessens, the boys and Jacob were glad to be getting back on the road home. It seemed not to take as long this way, though there was really very little difference in the time it was taking. Going home always seems to take less time than going away. The horse seemed to know that it would soon be back in familiar surroundings, too, and made the extra effort to keep up its speed. The boys were interested in some of the things they had seen on the way before, and paid more careful attention to some other things that now gripped their eyes. Jacob was more jovial and added an occasional light-hearted joke to his discussions with them. Thus the time passed, and before they knew it, they were back in Altona.

Chapter 15

Dorcas and the younger children were overjoyed to see them all back safely. The family had spent many a moment praying that nothing would happen to them along the way. Gerritt, though he enjoyed the company of the Derksens, knew that he needed to go into Hamburg to see his mother and sister, so he had been dropped off as they went through the city. He had some things on his mind, too.

Preparations for the trek went into high gear almost immediately. Jacob outlined to George Toews what would be needed, and the men began to seek the parts they would need for the windmill, and to construct what they could of the framework for it. The wagon factory went into production once again, producing the sturdier wagons that would be needed to haul the windmill parts, as well as other heavy items. One of the men searched for suitable draft horses, for they would need many more than they presently had. The Altona Mennonites subsidized this out of their reserve funds, as a part of what they considered their duty to their fellow believers. Many were staying in Altona, dreading any further trekking, but roughly half the group was intending to go east with Jacob.

Gerritt was asked to preach again quite soon after getting back, and he delivered another inspiring sermon. He, of course, sought out Suzie after the service, and spoke with her until her parents called her, and Martina called him, to go home. Gerritt, however, said that he needed to speak to George Toews, the Schultze, which he then did. He announced to him that he had decided to stay in Hamburg with his hosiery business and not go on the trek to Heubuden, and that he would be available to preach as the church in Altona needed. They took him up on that offer, and soon he was preaching almost every week. The Altona church was not aware at that time that this gifted young man would be with them for five decades to come, and that he would lead them through many a struggle with doctrine and with separatist groups. One person in the congregation, however, knew in her heart without having heard it from the Schultze, that this young man was going to be an important part of her life for many years to come.

The Derksen family also made preparations for their move. Items that were not needed until the next year were carefully cleaned and packed. Stored food needed to be crated or put into crocks for transport. Crates and crocks needed to be found for this. Dorcas moved forward with resolve and with skill in getting all the details ready. Not only did she look after her own adopted family, but she helped every other wife to organize packing, as well. Nothing could be left to chance, everything needed to be thought of beforehand and planned out carefully, so that no step in the process was overlooked. Dorcas managed all this with typical calmness and cheerfulness, so the families grew to love her and trust her judgment in all the myriad things that were to be done.

The children got more and more excited, as the winter blended slowly and fitfully into spring. They were going on a very long journey, and they would see many new things. Although this sometimes caused them to get in the way, Dorcas managed to keep them occupied in productive activities that would give her time to do the things she needed to accomplish on her own. By now, Joshua, Mary and Elizabeth, as well as Susan and Nicholas, were getting old enough to be of a little help for short times, and she planned ways to utilize their energies in helpful ways. The smaller children needed to be cared for, and she hired Lizzy to come in and help with that. This kept the sense of family togetherness alive, even though they came from very different genetic pools. Jonathan, Agnes, Willy and JJ were showered with all sorts of attention, and Lizzy had grown to be quite a capable leader, thinking of all sorts of interesting things in which they could be involved. Of course, JJ was mostly carried on the hip, but he seemed also to enjoy the antics of the others around him. Benjamin was fully involved with his father in the preparations for the move. He was strong and capable, and he enjoyed the physical work that this meant. Most of all, he enjoyed working closely with his father, whom he adored and sought to emulate. Gerritt showed up occasionally with his mother to complete the picture and add to the work force.

March had come, and most of the preparations had been made. A few last things were still to be purchased, as they were not generally available in the smaller cities further east, and they would be needed when they began to set up their village of Heubuden. True to the name Jacob had given to the location, the families would be building huts, or booths out of the native swamp grass, before more permanent structures could be built. For the booths, nothing would be needed, as the abundant grass would be utilized for every part of these simple constructions. It was for the building of permanent homes that more things would be needed. Stove parts were cast iron, so they were heavy. The remainder of the stove would be built of the local brick. Jacob had ordered bricks on his trip earlier, and they would be delivered to the site sometime after they had arrived, likely near the end of April. Horse-drawn land clearing machinery was found, as well as agricultural implements that would be used in putting the land to productive use, and these were dismantled for transport. Already some of the sturdy wagons were filling with these heavier items. The lighter wagons would be used for transporting the personal effects and the mothers and children. Again, as had been the case in their coming to Altona a few years before, the older children and younger men and women would be expected to walk behind the horses and wagons, carrying personal effects strapped to their backs. Sturdy shoes needed to be bought or made, as lighter footwear would quickly wear out on such a long journey. Home remedies needed to be assembled and packed, as there would be no doctors available along the way, nor would there be one nearby, once the group settled in Heubuden. A couple of the women were skilled as <u>Traichtmoacha</u>, or chiropractors and they were already in high demand, even in Altona.

Count von Schauenburg, who controlled Altona and the area surrounding the growing town, became aware that a sizable group of his Mennonites was planning to move from his domain to West Prussia, which was either under Polish domination or under the rival German group of Hohenzollerns. This caused alarm in the court. He was going to lose most of the tax revenues that he was now collecting, somewhat under the general heading of extortion, from them. Especially the recruitment tax, which was based on a head count, would be affected. He decided that this would not be practical for him at all, so he acted.

News of the decree came through George Toews, the Schultze, with whom the Count did his business. He in turn brought it to the community council, of which Jacob was once more a part.

> Be it known, that there shall be no move of any persons or groups of persons from one part of my domain to another nor any move to any location outside my domain without my express permission.

George read the statement to the group, who sat in stunned silence. Jacob had put so much work into preparations for the move, and now the Count was forbidding them to carry through on this venture. It was not hard to see the reasoning behind his sudden, callous move, but because it hit so close to home, it came as a cataclysmic blow.

No one spoke. Jacob, along with the others, sat looking down at his clenched fists on the table before him, his hands pulsing with the energy of tightening and loosening, with which he was releasing his inner frustrations. One by one, the men began to look at each other, a quizzical, almost pleading expression on each face. What were they to do now?

"We must obey the Count's ruling," Jacob broke the silence. "He believes that he will lose too much tax revenue, if we leave, and that is plainly the truth. I guess God wants us to continue to support him for now. Perhaps he will change his mind, if we are patient and wait for a more opportune time. In the meantime, we will go on as if we were intending to stay, we will plant our gardens and crops, and we will try to get some businesses going to sustain us. And we can begin the negotiations to leave, perhaps next year."

The men listened intently, nodding their heads here and there in agreement. George responded for all of them, "I agree with Jacob. We cannot fight the Count's decree. We can only begin to negotiate. I am aware of a group of Mennonites in Friesland that would like to come to Altona. Maybe we could negotiate on the basis that one group leaves and another group comes."

That seemed to please all of them somewhat. But, there were still questions.

"What is to say that the group from Friesland will be able to carry on the businesses we already have going?" one of the men asked.

"How do we know that those pesky Frieslanders will fit into our community, which has adopted the Flemish beliefs," another thought.

"How many of them are there?" one of Jacob's group of émigrés questioned. "There are twenty families planning to go. Are there more or less in the group that wants to come here?" Jacob replied with his own question.

Discussion continued for some time, as each of the leaders became more aware of the extent of the problem and the magnitude of the possible solution. It was not uncommon for large groups of Mennonites to resettle, some from the Low Countries and some from Flanders. Others from various areas of the northern Rhine valley and the plains of Lower Saxony were also looking to move out of areas of extreme tension. To be sure, the Thirty Years' War had put an end to capital punishment for having Anabaptist beliefs, but it had not put an end to the policies of oppression that faced them wherever they lived. Some rulers were more tolerant than others, so the tension was less conspicuous there, and Mennonites were drawn to live in areas where the tension was less obvious. They refused to participate in any community government except their own, but they paid the taxes required to placate the rulers of the principalities in which they resided. Since Germany was not yet a unified country, there were literally hundreds of such petty principalities to deal with. Even the Low Countries had just recently gained independence from the Holy Roman Empire to become an entity in their own right. Reformed Protestant Netherlands had thus been born, separating itself from Catholic Flanders, which remained under Spain.

Jacob came home to Dorcas and announced the Count's decree. That practical woman simply nodded and said, "We will begin to get ready to plant our garden and sow our grain, and to prepare for next winter. Perhaps we can go next year." Thus she seemed to divine Jacob's thoughts.

Jacob's thoughts, however, were deeply troubled. Since they had not been able to continue marketing their wagons through the merchants in Hamburg, who were now boycotting them, how were they to continue their enterprise profitably? They could convert the factory to produce other items of wood, but these would not be as profitable, and they would not sustain the community, as their former business had done. The brewery would have to continue to produce the money required for the recruitment tax, so there was no thought of expanding that.

George had mentioned that there was a group of Mennonites wanting to move to Altona. Perhaps they would need sturdy wagons. He would investigate the possibility of exporting the wagons directly to Friesland. In fact, it might be best to send Jacob to Holland, to see whether this was a possibility, and also to get a sense of what the issues might be in bringing in a large group of Mennonites from another place. Jacob's experience as a preacher in their church and also as a community leader would make him the best suited for this role. He came over to Jacob's house that evening with his proposal.

"But I have never been to the Low Countries," Jacob objected.

"You hadn't been to Prussia, either," countered George. "I think you would be the best one to go and meet the group that is contemplating a move in this direction, and since you have been heading up the wagon production, you are obviously the best one to check on possible markets."

"What do you think, Dorcas? Can you manage without me again?"

"Yes, I think you should go. God has kept us here for a purpose. It is now our job to find out what that purpose is. This seems to me to be an open door to find out His will." Dorcas' theology was extremely practical, as her solutions always were. She did not take a long time to think about such things, nor did she believe that the Christian life was supposed to be terribly spiritual. It was a practical life, to be enjoyed together in God's presence. What He provided was what was good, and it was our job to recognize the good in it.

"Should I take Benjamin with me again?" Jacob directed his question at Dorcas.

"I think you should, but you should also take Joshua. He is old enough to be of help to you, and it would be good for him to see where our ancestors came from," she said, simply.

"I guess that settles it," Jacob turned toward George. Together, they sipped on the hot coffee with cream that Dorcas had been preparing for them while they talked. "I will make preparations starting tomorrow, and within the week, we should be gone to Holland."

Chapter 16

"I thought it was flat near Altona," Joshua stated, amazed, "but this is like a table top."

"Yes, if it weren't for groves of trees, windmills and canals, there would hardly be anything to see at all," Benjamin responded eagerly. "I like seeing the boats going through the pastures and grain fields, though. It seems so . . ." and he couldn't think of the word to complete the sentence.

"Incongruous," Jacob filled in. "That means it doesn't seem to fit into what we would expect."

"That's right," said Joshua. "Incongrumous."

"Incongruous," Jacob corrected.

The boys practiced this new word several times before they could pronounce it properly, and then recounted other things that were incongruous in their experience. The sight of trading boats plying the many canals that cut through the countryside became a familiar sight quite soon. The windmills, mostly constructed to supply power for pumping water from the low-lying areas of reclaimed land, were also quickly absorbed into their experience. The construction of houses was very similar to what it was in all parts of lowland northern Germany, so they had seen similar-looking villages before. Benjamin could relate new things to others he had experienced on his journey to West Prussia, and he soon became the expert in describing these similarities to his younger brother.

The Mennonites had moved to other areas of Friesland, not centered any more in the area around Witmarsum, where Jacob's grandparents had originated, but scattered in villages all over northern Friesland and Groningen to the northeast. Another large group was centered in Waterland, much farther south. Jacob had a satchel of papers, which he consulted regularly, but unknown even to the boys, they were unimportant papers of general information, not specifically related to his mission at all. He had committed to memory the names and addresses of the people he was to see, leaving no material trace by which enemies could implicate others with him, should he be stopped and interrogated. The papers related simply to business items that would indicate that he was a businessman going about his routine activities, thus turning attention away from religious issues that might become delicate, should the wrong officials stop him for questioning. Unknown to Jacob, this tactic would be copied many times in later years, as God's people sought to escape oppression of one kind or another, while moving about in His work.

He found the first person he was seeking, Herman Banman, who seemed to be heading up the group from Friesland that wanted to immigrate to Altona. He lived in a small village somewhat off the beaten track, and carried on his small-scale farming operation from there, while preaching clandestinely in workshops and machine sheds around the area. He was aware of another group from Waterland that also wanted to join in the trek out of Holland. At the same time, he indicated that the Mennonites were thriving there, and the officials did not seem to be putting too much pressure on them, now that the United Provinces had become The Netherlands and were independent of the Holy Roman Emperor. Their reason for wanting to move was simply that they had adopted the Flemish beliefs in church discipline and were not acceptable to the Friesians that wanted to remain with their original beliefs on that issue. The group was comprised of a mixture of Friesians and Flemish immigrants, but practiced church discipline according to the Flemish tradition. The group from Waterland, he noted, was of the same persuasion and wished to emigrate for the same reason. Jacob was satisfied, then, that the people would fit into their group in Altona, who had also brought with them the Flemish tradition, which had been adopted by his grandfather and Menno in Wuestenfelde. George Toews would be pleased to hear that, as this seemed to be the major dividing theme among the Mennonites, and it was not easily settled locally, except by going their separate ways.

As for the subject of wagons, this seemed to be of great interest to Herman Banman. They were not as far into the details of planning their trek out of the country as Jacob's group was in their planning, so it had not come up in the discussions with his compatriots. He would be meeting with them the night after his meeting with Jacob, so an answer might quickly be forthcoming. In the meantime, he asked whether Jacob would mind preaching in a meeting scheduled for that evening. Jacob agreed, looking at his boys, who grimaced appropriately, knowing that they would have heard this sermon before, but secretly glad that their father was once again doing what he loved to do.

The meeting that evening allowed Jacob to meet a number of those who planned to emigrate. He did not tell them of the restriction that had been placed on his group that planned to leave Altona, but indicated that they would be welcome to join the group that was there, if they could find ways of providing for themselves in the tight circumstances they found themselves in. For the Mennonites in Holland, this had been the state of life for the past century, so it did not dampen their enthusiasm one bit. His sons did not spoil his sermon by reacting negatively, for which he rewarded them with a big smile after he was finished.

After travelling to several other villages and meeting with other Mennonites there, Jacob and his boys felt they had a good grasp of what their fellow believers were going through. They realized also that the issues they faced in Altona were faced by other Mennonites from Friesland to East Prussia. Everywhere they had fled, they were squeezed into a tight mold between religious prejudice and political expediency.

Jacob and his sons left Friesland early one morning, going around the great inland sea that separated Friesland from southern Holland. It took nearly a week for them to reach Waterland along the southern coast, crossing numerous bridges and taking numerous ferries in order to get there. When they arrived at the next place that Jacob had in his memory, they found the house where they were to stay. Isaac DeFehr met them with warm embraces and got his sons to take the horse and carriage to the barn, instructing them to feed the animal and water it, and to check the carriage and the harness, in case any repairs were needed. He, in turn, pulled Jacob and the boys into the house, where his wife was preparing a good meal that they were just going to sit down to. She was able without too much fuss to add to it, realizing that there would be additional mouths to feed. Place was quickly made for the guests, and the meal brought to the table, just as her sons got back from the barn.

Conversation at the table revolved around family questions, so that by the end of the meal, each understood quite a bit about the other. The situations in which they lived were also discussed quite freely, and Jacob soon discovered that these Waterlanders were mostly made up of Flemish refugees, some from a generation or two ago, who were now feeling that they wished to start a new life in Altona, where they had heard many of their fellow believers had found permanent refuge. Jacob told them of their coming <u>en masse</u> from Wuestenfelde three years before, as the Catholic army was poised to come in and destroy the village. Their group had grown following the time that Menno had lived in their midst, but could not stay, because they refused to defend their property against the coming army. The few Mennonites in Altona had welcomed them with open arms, and the Counts von Schauenburg had taken them in, not offering too much resistance, because they wanted good workers for their town. As the war had gone on around them, though, the Mennonites had been forced to pay the exorbitant recruitment tax, in order to avoid having their young men drafted into the local Protestant army units by the King of Denmark, to fight the Catholics. When the Protestant armies capitulated in one battle after another, Christian IV had been forced to sign a peace treaty, in which he was forced to stay out of the war from that point on. Jacob, having been on the community council, had been privy to all that went on around them. He did not tell them of his trip to West Prussia, and he had told his boys not to mention it either, for that would bring a whole new line of questions into play, which he was not prepared to answer at this time. Only the matter of a market for their wagons and their acceptance of émigrés from Holland were to be the topics of discussion. Even the convoluted state of his family was only mentioned as a necessity, due to deaths of another set of parents and of his wife, removing any suspicions of trouble beyond the normal.

Again, Jacob was asked to preach, and in the hidden meetings he met many of the families that wanted to emigrate to Altona. It seemed to him to be quite a healthy mix of people, some with experience in city occupations, and some with experience in skilled trades. Some had experience in draining swamps and in reclaiming land from the sea, along with windmill building and utilization. They would perhaps become valuable additions to his group's plans for moving on to Heubuden, but he did not pursue that at this time. Again, his boys sat patiently through the repeated sermons from before, interested more in the young people from the families that might be coming to join them in Altona, especially some of the young women, who looked at them from under their shawls with coquettish smiles and smiling eyes.

Isaac DeFehr had a surprise in store for Jacob and the boys. Just before they were ready to pack up and leave to return to Altona, he asked them to bring their carriage around to a shed behind his barn. Curious, Jacob steered his horse to the shed's doorway. Isaac went in and, one by one, he brought out six beehive colonies, hibernating through the winter. Placing them in the baggage area of the carriage, he smiled and wished Jacob and the boys success in honey-production during the coming summer. Neither Jacob nor his boys realized what this would mean for the community in Altona. At the time, their concern was mainly where to place their baggage, now that the space for it was taken by the beehives.

The trip from Waterland to Altona took about the same time as it had to reach Friesland from Altona. Dorcas and the younger ones were overjoyed to see them back, and Jacob could hardly wait to report back to George Toews and the community leadership. The beehives would need to be cared for and placed where the bees could gather the most pollen and nectar possible; someone would have to be found who understood what was involved, for Jacob did not. They could build wagons once more, as these were needed by both Dutch groups immediately, even though neither was yet ready to begin its move to Altona. Both groups felt that it might be best to wait until autumn to make their move. This would also suit the group in Altona, for it would give them time to make the necessary arrangements for housing, to clear their arrival with town officials and the Count, and to enlarge their facilities for worship.

It would, perhaps, be a hindrance in their negotiations with the Count for permission for a group to leave Altona in spring, but Jacob believed that it would rather be a help, as he could indicate to the Count that he would not be losing valuable workers to pay the recruitment tax, but simply replacing one with the other. The men on the council went to work immediately, making decisions to revive the wagon factory's production. The machinery that had been packed away was once more brought out and re-installed, and necessary inventory was ordered, so that production could be begun as soon as possible. Idle men were once more happily at work, and Jacob's life took on more of a routine. Many questions were asked as to who could manage the beekeeping, and for the first week, no one knew of anyone that had any experience in this art. Fortunately for all, the bees remained dormant.

Sunday came, and with it came the regular church service. Since this was the only time that the entire community, so to speak, assembled together at one time, it was also a time when public announcements could be made for all to hear. George Toews was asked to make a plea about beekeeping, to see if anyone knew anyone that might have some knowledge of this valuable community skill. To everyone's surprise, Martina stood up and said that her father had kept bees, and that she had been his helper all through her growing up years. She would be happy to help the community manage its new industry.

Chapter 17

The seasons were marked by their special activities. The spring field work and seeding came along with the preparation and planting of the gardens. Carefully tended seedlings that had been started on window sills were set out into the cultivated garden soil. Seeds that had been dried with practiced skill were scattered in rows measured off with sticks and string and dug with guided hoes. Pails of water were brought to the garden plot to water the tender cabbage, Brussels sprouts and cauliflower transplants that now formed straight rows. Potatoes were cut into chunks, each having at least two eyes that might sprout, were pushed down into the soft, moist and hilled earth in measured intervals. The men that were in charge of seeding the grain crops carefully plowed the still-moist fields, and then harrowed them down to break up the chunks formed by the plowshare. Seeds were broadcast in the time-honored way of walking down the fields in straight lines, while dipping the hand in the basket or bag of seed slung over the shoulders in measured intervals, and flinging the handful of seeds rhythmically out onto the prepared field. The harrows were once more pulled over the seeded field, to imbed the seeds into the rich soil. The men had done all they could; it was now up to God to water the seeds and make them sprout. Prayers to that effect went up in the Sunday service, when everyone stopped work and met together for worship and intercession. In the meantime, Martina, with a few helpers that had been recruited for the task and trained by her, moved the beehives out of their storage facility to areas that would soon have ample blossoms for their foraging. The hives had been checked to make sure the queen was alive in each, and that the worker bees had survived the winter. Martina and her helpers began to anticipate the blessing that this would be to the Mennonite community in Altona.

When the spring work was finished, Jacob called his crew together again, and the wagon factory once more went into production. The Mennonites in Holland would need sturdy wagons for their move to Altona, so those took precedence over carriages, which were designed for transporting people more comfortably. To be sure, that only meant that they had a wooden seat with a low back on them. They still did not have springs on the axles, and the tires were still of molded iron, heat formed and cooled onto the wooden wheels. There was no covering over the passengers or the driver, nor was the baggage protected from the elements. Bearings were still of wood, greased with pork fat. When it could be obtained, some might be lubricated with raw bitumen, but the sources were not plentiful, and bitumen was expensive.

Even plows had been made mostly of wood, with a blade of iron fastened to the wooden board that formed the plowshare. Jacob talked with his blacksmiths and devised a way of molding the plowshare out of a single piece of flat iron. They were often pulled by teams of oxen, who moved slowly but patiently along the furrow, guided by the calls and prods of the plowman. Harrows were simply constructed of pointed pegs set into a lattice of hardwood slats and pulled by a team of horses. It took all a good agile man could do to keep up with them for an extended length of time, for horses moved much faster than oxen. The size of the field that could be plowed by a team of oxen pulling a single plow share in one morning was called a <u>Morgen</u>, which meant morning. Fields were commonly measured in terms of <u>Morgen</u>, which in German is both singular and plural. The Mennonite community held their grain fields in common in Altona, because the whole group needed the produce from them, and because no one family had the resources with which to do the farming operations. The few that had rented land from nearby farmers had been forced over the past couple of years to return the land, for it was not deemed wise to allow a member of a sect to be involved in food production for the local German community. This was another way in which the governing officials limited both Jews and Mennonites, since neither fitted well into the dominant society. The Jews went into commerce, and the Mennonites went into a limited form of communal living, mostly to work in skilled trades, both as a response to the limitations placed on them during this time.

Jacob was in his element. He was eminently satisfied with the way their society functioned. He never had any sense of greed or envy that would motivate him to seek advancement for himself. Life was to be lived for the community, not for the individual. He believed that this is what the Bible taught, and he gladly practiced it in all its varied applications. Only family life was private, and that privacy was taken for granted. But even that was influenced by the communal nature of Mennonite life, which was always lived out in the context of fleeing, or hiding, or living under restrictions.

One day Jacob and Dorcas were sitting alone by their table. Jacob leaned over, took her hand in his, looked directly into her eyes and said tenderly, "I know you would stay here regardless of what I did, just to be a help, but I want you to know that I appreciate your spirit very much. I also know that our family could not do without you anymore, and I want you to know that this is very important to me personally. You are my kin, and I know it isn't common for this to happen, but it does happen occasionally, that cousins marry. Would you marry me?"

The poor woman didn't know what to say. She had never talked with a man before about personal feelings, and she had never had an interest in any man before. She wrung her hands in her apron and brought it up to cover her blushing face, and then looked furtively at the waiting man, out of whose hands she had wrung hers.

"Of course I'll stay, Jacob. I just don't know what to say about changing our relationship of one that is family to one that is, well, more than just family," she stammered.

"I will not press you for an answer right now, Dorcas, but I want you to know that I have come to love you as dearly as I ever loved Rebekah," Jacob continued tenderly.

"And I guess I've grown to love you, too, Jacob," she replied, drying her eyes with her apron and wiping a stray grey hair from her face, "I think I could fit in as easily as your wife as I have fitted in as your nanny, I guess. I respect how you have treated me, and I admired the tenderness you showed toward Martina, during your very difficult period with her. Yes, I guess I'll accept your proposal and marry you. I suspect we won't be able to have children anymore, though, if that is what you were hoping."

"Thank you, Dorcas, for accepting me. I know you had already accepted the family long ago. Now we will be complete as a family. Whether we have more children together or not, I really don't care. I want the comfort of knowing that we are doing the right thing for each other, and the realization that we are there for each other, regardless of what happens. I will see if the Elder is coming soon, so we can take care of our new business together." His eyes twinkled as he said it, realizing just then that this was precisely what he had said to Martina. Somehow, he felt very different about this venture.

Jacob, as part of the leading council of men, guided by George Toews, the Schultze, made decisions that were binding on each man and each family in the Mennonite community. Should someone not wish to be submissive, it was considered to be a matter of church, as well as community, discipline. Occasionally, someone would be found out to have been guided by personal greed or sense of hoarding, and would be brought up before the council of leaders, who also functioned as the governing board of the church. Their discipline was harsh, for they believed in the Flemish guidelines of duty to the community, rather than individual freedom, as the Friesian Mennonites practiced. If a person was excommunicated from the church, he or she was automatically shunned by the community, and banned from any participation in community life, including working in any community projects, as well as from participating in any part of the church. Although no one could check this for certain, the expectation was that the spouse would cease any conjugal relationships with the shunned person. Needless to say, there was not a great deal of disciplinary action required to keep the community functioning fairly smoothly together. Rebellion mostly took the form of gossip and backbiting. The lasting forms of Mennonite society were taking shape in the forge of Church persecution and political restriction, with the basic teachings of Menno and the Bible guiding the various groups scattered over northern Europe.

Martina returned to the church, confessing that she had been quite rebellious for a time following her husband's death, and that her "affair" with Jacob had been part of that rebellion. The Mennonite leaders forgave her, and she took her regular place once more on the hard backless benches that were set out each Sunday in the wagon factory for the church services. She continued her job in the university library, where she earned enough to maintain her house in Hamburg and help her daughter with her education. She continued to study privately with a professor, and she managed the beekeeping of the community with consummate, loving skill and care. Gerritt's hosiery empire had grown to proportions talked about throughout the Hanseatic ports. He had heard about a knitting frame developed by a British preacher, Reverend William Lee in 1589, and had imported several of these frames from Paris, where the inventor had settled. After a short time of experimentation and training, Gerritt's workers were able to produce ample stockings for the Baltic trade. Because he did not travel extensively, but remained in his office in Hamburg, he also preached more and more, and the people learned to love their young speaker. His relationship with Suzie grew as she was able to recover from her traumatic experience of three years earlier. This, in turn, resulted in Jonathan and Susan Dyck becoming less stringent in their expectations of others, for they were now relaxed as to their daughter's future prospects. Lizzy began her studies at the university in preparation for becoming a medical doctor.

Dorcas managed the household as a good mother would. The small children were growing up and going to school, except JJ, who was still at home. He, too, was showing signs of being a precocious child, learning things quickly by emulation of his many older siblings. Benjamin and Joshua both worked in the wagon factory, Benjamin as an apprentice in the carpentry area, and Joshua learning accounting. Dorcas used her freedom to get involved in the community, helping families with a sick mother, or caring for an aged matriarch.

The beehives were a timely gift. The six hives produced very well, once the flowers came out. Some fields had been sown to clover, and these blossoms produced exquisite-tasting honey. There was enough to provide each of the Mennonite families with a sufficient supply, if they were careful in how they rationed it over the winter. Martina taught her crew, all of whom worked only part-time in this enterprise, what was required in caring for the bee colonies, how to maintain the hives, how to extract the honey, how to provide for the colony's needs over the next winter, and how to store the honey. With this added community responsibility, she was in her element, feeling important in a useful sort of way, no longer a drain on their society as a poor widow with no interest in the practical thinking that other women exhibited.

The Lord's timing is sometimes not in synchronization with human timing. Jacob found it so in autumn, just before the harvest. One day, George Toews brought a Jewish businessman from Hamburg to him at the wagon factory, and introduced him as having an interest in the types of wagons they were producing. Jacob took him through the plant, showing him the special features that made their wagons better than the competitors' products. The man seemed very interested in everything that he saw, and he asked about special adaptations that might be possible, to make the wagons useful for specific types of loads. At long last, when he and Jacob were alone together, the man got right to the point of his visit. He wanted to order ten of their most durable wagons, because he was expanding his business to include delivery of coal to households and businesses in Hamburg. Many of these premises had had new furnaces installed, that operated with coal as fuel, rather than wood, as had formerly been the case. The coal was shipped by barge down the Ruhr River, down the Rhine, and then tugged back up the Elbe to Hamburg, where it could be distributed. Herr Morgenstern's business, which he was adding to his already prosperous dray service, was to be this distribution network. He would need wagon boxes that were designed to maximize the amount of coal that could be hauled. He also asked whether the Mennonite community had any horses that he could buy, but here Jacob had to inform him that they only had enough for their own use, and that they might, in fact be needing some more themselves. He was going to try going to the army; perhaps they had horses that they no longer needed, now that relative peace had settled on the area. Herr Morgenstern thought this might be a good idea, and he would also try that approach. Papers signed, a deposit left with Jacob, the businessman left, and Jacob whistled in unbelief at this sudden positive turn of events. When he told the workers in the wagon factory, they also whistled at the good news. Before long, they were busily engaged in constructing these wagons, along with the ones they knew they needed for Holland, as well as the ones they would need to bring in their own harvest and then prepare for the eventual trek to West Prussia. God seemed to be smiling on them.

Negotiations with Count von Schauenburg were difficult. He was not sure he wanted to keep as many Mennonites in his realm as there were at present, but he certainly did not want to lose the recruitment tax revenue he was presently receiving from those that lived in Altona. He, in fact, threatened to add another tax to their already scandalous burden. To this, Jacob and his group simply replied that they would then leave, even without the Count's permission. That, of course, would leave the remaining ones to pay the entire levy, which would have been impossible. Jacob presented letters from the two groups in Holland, begging for permission to settle in Altona. These two groups would more than offset the group that intended to leave. Jacob knew that some from this group might also want to extend their trek all the way to West Prussia, as well. Although he did not mention this specifically in his negotiations, he was careful to state his case in such a way as to make it possible for them to choose this option, should they so desire.

An agreement was reached, by which each household that left would be required to pay an additional fee to the Count for that privilege, and the recruitment tax would remain as it was. If any other Mennonites came to Altona, they would be required to pay the recruitment tax, even if they only remained for a short time before leaving again. They would also have to pay for the privilege of leaving, once they were in the Count's realm. That meant that it would be advantageous, if it were possible, to have them settle in Hamburg, rather than Altona, to avoid settling in the Count's territory. Jacob then began negotiations with the city fathers of Hamburg, seeking the best possible deal there.

The Lutheran merchants of Hamburg, as well as the Jews, were not happy with the prospects of a competitive group on their doorstep, so they stonewalled the negotiations, appealing to the city fathers, as well. Jacob seemed not to be able to get anywhere with them. He called on Gerritt to help him in these negotiations. That young merchant had a good reputation in the city, and he carried considerable influence with the city fathers, who were amazed at his early business success. Together, the Mennonite leader and the young businessman were able to negotiate a suitable agreement for the Mennonites from Holland. The question now was, would they be happy to move directly to the biggest city in northern Europe, or had they set their hearts on living in the town of Altona on its fringe?

Summer wore on into fall, and the harvest was in full swing. The bees had produced an ample crop of honey, and Martina guided her crew in the extraction process, as well as the storage of viable colonies over the winter. What she had not learned, she was able to find out through books in the library in which she worked, and the process proceeded with consummate efficiency. Many crocks were required to store the honey, taking away from the number available for sauerkraut. That meant that more needed to be bought from the local potters, thus providing them with unexpected income.

Gardens produced abundantly, and the harvest from these plots was also taken in by the women and preserved for the winter, while the men were on duty in the grain fields, wielding their sickles and binding sheaves in the hot sunshine, and drying them in shocks awaiting their pickup by wagons and teams. Threshing was accomplished on a hard floor, with flails, brooms and baskets in the wind. Hay had been brought in earlier and stored in the barns for the winter. The livestock would be well provided for, as would the Mennonite community. There was even enough for the incoming groups from Holland, who would not have the opportunity to bring much with them.

Once the harvest was in and all the preparation work for winter had been done, the men on Jacob's crew got to work on wagon-building in earnest. They had to get many wagons done for Herr Morgenstern, before the season for heating came, and they needed many more to ship to Holland, in preparation for the trek of the groups to join them. Jacob began the search for the extra horses they would need for the trek eastward. Mecklenburgers were the kind most common in that area, and their purple-colored hair made them an attractive sight. He bought a number of teams from local Jewish middlemen. Apparently they had been able to buy them up from the armies that no longer needed them. Jacob was surprised to see his old team, that he had sold to the agent connected with the army, so he bought them back. Oxen would also be used, and he kept his eye out for especially strong and well-behaved teams of the great cattle. The Jewish merchants were able to get him as many pairs as he needed. The extra feed they had collected in the good harvest would provide for them over the winter. Now Jacob needed to find housing for all of the new animals. This was accomplished when another local business could no longer continue, and the building became available to him. He brought his crew over for a few days, and they quickly converted the old business premises to a large barn, with open stalls, where either the oxen or the horses could be stabled. Feeding and cleaning was not as easy as in a standard barn arrangement, but it would do for this winter.

Chapter 18

The arrival of the two groups from Holland was handled much more easily than the arrival of the group from Wuestenfelde had been. There was a much larger group available to greet them and provide for their immediate needs. Housing had been found for everyone. It was not fancy, and in some cases, it was too small for the family that arrived. Information had not been accurate in some cases, so there were some adjustments to be made. Dorcas proved to be the efficient and caring hostess to all the families that came. Her caring attitude and keen, practiced eye were put to good use during the first week of their settling in. She was able to inform Jacob quickly of individual needs, which he and his crew were able to meet. Martina also provided valuable contacts, sometimes through her son or daughter, and sometimes on her own. Everyone in the Mennonite community shared in the trials and the joys of helping their new neighbours and fellow believers.

The first Sunday service came a few days after the groups had arrived, and it was very special to see the greatly enlarged group worshiping together for the first time. Jacob was asked to speak at this service, and he brought a warm message of welcome and hope to the entire group. Being historically minded, he traced their common background of persecution due to their faith and reminded them all, that God worked in every one of these circumstances to perfect his Church, which was the whole body of Christ in the entire world. He reminded them that they had fellow believers back in Holland, in other parts of Germany, and over in Royal and East Prussia, as well. He had even heard that some Mennonites from Switzerland, the Black Forest and the Palatinate had sailed over to America, in hopes that their beliefs would be protected in the New World. He based his message on the passages in the gospels where Jesus reminded His disciples of the hatred of the world toward Him and His followers, so it was to be expected that persecution would drive them out of the influence of the world. He showed them that persecution in the early church in the book of Acts had helped to spread the gospel to the ends of the Roman world, and that their present situation would result in many others coming into fellowship with Christ through their faithfulness. At the end of the message, he made a plea for others to join their planned trek to Prussia in spring. This was the first time that the Hollanders had heard about this plan, so it created quite a buzz among them after the service.

    A church potluck had been planned, and the families that had been there for the past three and a half years brought enough for all the others, as well. The church was cleared of benches, making an area where tables could be set up on sawhorses, and the baskets and pots with their delectable aromas could be displayed. Enough dishes and utensils had been brought, as well, so that everyone could partake together. A new fad at this time was the fork, which had recently been introduced from Italy. The Hollanders thought this was a unique invention, but they preferred to use their fingers, saying that these had been invented long before forks. Besides, it was delicious to be able to lick the fingers after they had been covered in sauce, while dipping their bread. As Dorcas looked around, she saw that their original refugees also preferred their fingers. Only the younger ones grabbed the new plaything and quickly adapted their eating to its use, so most of the forks were left untouched. Conversation naturally drifted to the proposed trek east, and many of the new émigrés were becoming convinced that they might actually be interested in joining Jacob's group in spring. For the moment, however, all spirits were light, and the new settlers felt the warmth of their hosts' welcome.

Because the new group had to find housing in Hamburg, their welcome was dependent on the whims of the Hanseatic businessmen that ran the city. When they became aware of the number of Mennonites in their midst, they sought ways to discourage them from remaining. The persecutions of the previous century were no longer tolerated by society, so more subtle legal pressures were brought to bear on them. New taxes were concocted, laying a heavy burden on the Mennonite community, which was taking responsibility for all the taxes levied, both in Hamburg and in Altona. They looked around at surrounding areas, but found that the same rulers controlled them, so that was not an option. They simply had to increase production in their various enterprises, to satisfy the money-lust of their authorities or find new businesses to generate more income.

George Toews and Jacob Derksen found themselves, together with the other community leaders, constantly negotiating with city officials, who came regularly with new demands on them. Demand for their wagons was great, and they increased production. Cloth continued to sell well, particularly when the new Mennonite settlers introduced silk and linen into their wares. The new-found post-war prosperity brought a demand among the merchant families for high quality luxury goods. The Dutch East India Company was the world's great trader in the 17th Century, and they brought spices from far eastern ports to Europe. The Mennonites' connection with Holland helped them to corner the market on spices among the Hanseatic cities, and this brought in new wealth, allowing them to pay the exorbitant demands of Hamburg's city council and Altona's Count von Schauenburg. It did make the thought of emigrating farther east to Prussia much more attractive, though, for both those who had come from Wuestenfelde and those who had recently arrived directly from Holland.

Jacob continued to make plans for the planned trek to Heubuden. Knowing that this would involve a complete new start, both as agricultural pilgrims and as astute businessmen, his preparations included both implements for breaking up new soil, as well as for continued agricultural pursuits. Manufacture was also considered, but since his present industries were already supplying the Hanseatic ports, including Danzig, there would be little profit in bringing them along. New items must be found for manufacture, items that would fit into the patterns of life farther east, and that could be used in the more primitive society around them there. He consulted with Gerritt about possibilities, and talked with Martina about possibly taking honey production into their new area.

Jacob was a builder, and his own bent was to think about construction, as well as the finished products that would complete such projects. *My grandfather was a brick maker and bricklayer; perhaps there will be opportunity for such an industry in Prussia.* That appealed to him. *Blacksmithing has also become part of the list of skilled trades that might be available to our new community, and it is a valuable one. There will be cattle and horses – perhaps tanning can be added, and work with leather. Shoemaking might be possible. Eric Bartsch is a shoemaker in Altona now, and he might be persuaded to come along. Martina's knowledge of beekeeping has brought her back into a tolerated fellowship with the Mennonites, but her intellectual and artistic bents make her difficult to understand. Would Martina be interested in going east? Will her children allow her to go, if she is interested? Has she trained her crew well enough that one of them would be able to introduce beekeeping into the new community?* So Jacob's mind flitted from one creative idea to another. Ever practical, the thought of Mennonites entering the arts never entered Jacob's mind. It would have offended him, if it had, for the arts were viewed as something invented by the devil to distract under-employed people from useful involvement in the community. Always the community came first. Individual interests were to be held subservient to the needs of the community.

"I think we should bring bees with us to Heubuden," Jacob began after church one Sunday, addressing Martina. "Do you have anyone that you could recommend as one who would be able to introduce this industry to the new community?"

"Are you asking me to move with you?" she guessed at his motives.

"Well, that would be one possibility, I'll admit, but if you know of someone else who could head it up, that would also be fine," he responded with a smile.

"I would think you wouldn't want me around anymore," she countered, also twisting her large square face into an unaccustomed smile. She brushed a stray greying hair from her small, cold blue eyes, and looked hard at Jacob.

"Don't get me wrong, Martina, I have no further interest in marrying you, but I also don't have anything against you, even though we don't fit together as a married couple," Jacob clarified.

"I didn't really think so, Jacob, but I couldn't resist teasing you a little. You always seem so intense and so absorbed in your plans, you never have a smile on your face."

Jacob absorbed this new attack on his personality with a lot of patience and forbearance. Although it stung, he knew she was right in her assessment of him. He tended to be dour, without a smile and without totally concentrating on the people he was speaking with. His mind seemed preoccupied all the time with other things.

"There doesn't seem to be any useful argument against that," he admitted. "Perhaps I should take up jousting with the Count?"

"You can play mentally, too, not just physically, and have just as much fun doing it," she suggested. "I read a lot, and that keeps me in tune with the thoughts of the world around me. Maybe you should take up reading."

"Maybe we should get back to the original topic of discussion. Do you know of anyone that might come along to Heubuden as our beekeeper, or do I have to learn that from you?" he brought the subject back to his thoughts.

"My crew were all good workers and very helpful, but none of them could be considered as having learned the trade well enough to be dependable leaders in a new situation. They can continue to look after the hives here, but I doubt that they could handle setting up a new colony of bees elsewhere."

"That seems to leave only one option open for us, doesn't it? Unless you want to teach me over the winter, and that would be very impractical, I would think," Jacob was now the one that teased. Apparently he had learned one thing from her, and very quickly, at that.

"I'll consider moving, but I have to think about my children, and I know that Gerritt will not leave his business here, nor does he want to stop being the preacher, especially with his new interest in Suzie. Lizzy's interests in becoming a doctor are very strong, and I don't want to leave her here alone," she said thoughtfully. "Perhaps I could visit for a time, when it is right to put out the hives, and then later, when it is time to gather in the honey and store the bees over the winter. That would be a nice break from my routine work in Hamburg."

For Jacob, it was important that his world, as he was planning it, would be well-rounded, whole, and caring. Martina's willingness to make special trips to Heubuden to supervise the beekeeping indicated to him something of all of these qualities. He went home happy and contented. Dorcas noticed this, and smiled. His children noticed that he was wearing a smile, too, and they settled contentedly into their meal. Dreams of a new life in Heubuden began dancing around in everyone's head. It would be a good life, without the tensions of the past or the present. It would be fulfilling, in that everyone would have a useful place in their new society. They would be able to practice their dearly-held beliefs without the constant pressure of persecution or high taxes. Yes, life would be good in Heubuden. But, there was something else that occupied Jacob's mind just now.

"Auntie Dorcas and I will be married next week, when the Elder comes to town," he announced. "We will go to the Standesamt tomorrow to sign the papers there and go through the legal ceremony, and then we will have a church wedding."

Excitement was strong around the table. Everyone rejoiced over the good news. Dorcas, for whom the timing of her wedding was just as much news as for the children, took it in stride.

"Come, children, we must get busy in planning our wedding," she gathered them together and began to list off the things that needed to be done and who would best do them. She was involving all her accumulated children in her own wedding!

Chapter 19

Spring was fast approaching, when Jacob planned to begin the trek to the East. That made it all the more surprising, when George came to him one day and said, "Jacob, I am afraid the Count has once more found a way to delay your going to Prussia. I think he just likes the idea that he has all of the new Hollanders here, all paying into the recruitment tax, so he has issued a new decree forbidding anyone to leave the county for the next year. He is also demanding that the recruitment tax now be paid on a per-person basis, instead of a lump sum for the whole group. He is satisfied to receive payment in beer, as before, but we are going to have to increase production in the brewery to make that possible."

Jacob stood in stunned silence. Another delay, for no apparent reason, except to extort more money out of the Mennonites. Like all German nobility, the Counts von Schauenburg were experts at finding ways to bring more into their coffers, but this was becoming intolerable. Not knowing what else to say, Jacob shrugged his shoulders and went on with his work at the wagon factory.

That evening he came home to Dorcas and the children with a sad countenance and dropped gaze. "What is the matter with you," asked his new wife. "You look as though you have been pushed through the sausage stuffer."

"I feel as though I have been put through the meat grinder and the sausage stuffer all at the same time," he replied dejectedly. "The Count has forbidden us to go to Prussia, and he has changed the recruitment tax, so that even the Hollanders have to pay it. We have to double production in the brewery, just to meet his new demands."

"Well, let's have supper, Jacob, and maybe that will help us think through the problem better. Perhaps the Lord will show us a way to get around the demand, or to meet it in a new way," Dorcas replied. Ever the practical one, as well as the trusting one, she had a deep faith that God was leading them. It was simply a matter of determining what He was suggesting for this situation.

Jacob shrugged his shoulders and cocked his head in surrender. He had exhausted all the ideas that he might have had quite some time ago, and this seemed to him to be just another blow to his already troubled mind. He washed his hands and face, dried them on the towel beside the basin, and took his accustomed place at the head of the table. Looking down the long bench beside him, he could not help but notice that Benjamin and Joshua were becoming quite grown-up looking. Benjamin's upper lip was sporting a fine dark line of hair, and Joshua's blond hair continued down his temples to nearly the bottom of his chin. My, how the children have grown, he thought.

Bowing his head, he began quite unaccustomedly, to pray out loud, "Dear God, you have been very good to our family. You have given us a wonderful mother, and we have a comfortable home. You have kept us in safety for over three years, and you have been with us through many difficult circumstances. We are seeking to follow your Word and to obey it in every way, but our leaders continue to find ways to take from us every blessing you give to us. Lord, please teach us what we are to do now. Thank you for this wonderful family. Thank you for the wonderful woman that has prepared our meal today, and thank you for the meal that you have provided for us. Amen"

Although the children had never heard their father pray out loud, it did not seem to surprise them in the least. They bowed their heads reverently, as they were accustomed to doing, and simply listened to his prayer instead of reciting their own memorized table grace in their minds, as they usually did. What surprised them was the fact that, when Jacob was finished, Dorcas began to pray.

"Dear Father in heaven, I am indeed thankful for your leading me to this family. I thank you even more, that you allowed me to remain in the Derksen family, and that you have given me such a wonderful husband and such wonderful children. Dear Father, you have heard what the Count has said, and you know the pressures we are living under. You can show us what we can do to meet his demands, and you know why we are to stay this extra year in Altona. Thank you, Father, for allowing me the privilege at my age to become a mother in my own right. Hallelujah!"

Jacob and the children completely missed the point of what she prayed. They were so surprised at her sudden contribution that the import of what she had just imparted to them went completely past them without their comprehending what she meant. Instead, Benjamin decided that, if the others were praying out loud, then he probably should, too.

"God, we thank you for our family. Thank you for bringing Mama Dorcas to us. Thank you for this tasty food. Amen," he said.

Joshua, feeling somewhat pressured to pray, but not being confident of his ability to, looked pleadingly at his father. Jacob sensed his hesitation and simply said loudly, "Amen." At this moment, he began to wonder what it was that Dorcas had meant by her final thought that had elicited her paean of praise. He looked at her quizzically, as she calmly began dishing up the plates. She had a whimsical smile on her face, and did not look at him.

When all the plates had been dished up and everyone was eating heartily, she looked Jacob squarely in the eye with a mischievous twinkle in hers. He stared at her hard, trying to decipher that unaccustomed look. Finally, he could stand it no longer.

"Do you have a secret way for us to meet the Count's demand?" he asked, shaking his head and raising his shoulders in mock dejection.

"Not at the moment, but I do have something that I would like to share. We are going to have a baby."

Jacob almost lost his balance, even though he sat on a fairly substantial chair. This was not something that he had thought of, since Dorcas was at an age when women generally stop bearing children. He sat there in stunned silence, looking first at her and then at the children around the table. All of them were similarly stunned, but then they began a loud cheer. Jacob, finally realizing that Dorcas was announcing her pregnancy to all of them, joined in the cheer, then pulled her head closer and kissed her fervently. This kind of public display of affection was also unaccustomed in the family, so another chorus went up from the cheering section.

"Well, I guess that is a good reason why we should stay here for another year," Jacob was finally able to speak. "I propose that we celebrate by having some of the dried fruit that we have in our crocks for dessert tonight." Another cheer told him that this suggestion was well received, and the meal went on with friendly banter and good wishes to Dorcas. This dutiful woman, as she took it to be her role as wife and mother, began to rise from her chair to go get the fruit, but Jacob interrupted her.

"Mary, would you please get the crock with the fruit. We must protect Mother, and not let her work so hard, now that she is carrying a baby." Dorcas sat back down, fussed with her apron and smiled at Jacob, then at the whole family, relaxing while Mary quickly went for the dessert. The boys took their cue from this and offered to help with the supper cleanup, something that wouldn't have crossed their minds a day before.

"Well, since we have so much time to talk, now that the children are busy doing all the work I would have been doing, except for your kind intervention, Jacob, let's discuss what we must do to raise the necessary money for the Count. Here are just a few ideas that came to me during supper: What about the whaling industry? Is it doing better, so that its contribution to the general fund could be greater? The same goes for the cloth merchants, weavers and spinners. What about the blacksmith shop, can it begin producing other things of use? Then, too, we have many people here, but no one of us runs a general store. That might be an idea. What about a bakery? Some of our baked goods from Holland and Flanders might be interesting to the Germans in Altona and Hamburg. I think our Mennonite <u>Wurst</u> would also sell well among the Germans. Does that give you enough ideas?" Dorcas was in rare form this evening, now that she had shared her little secret with the family, and her thoughts tumbled over one another in their haste to get out.

"Whoa, there," replied Jacob in mock defeat, "I haven't had time to think about the first idea you stated – what was it now, whaling, I think? Yes, we can pick up some extra cash there; they have had a good year. Cloth? It has been pretty steady, and Gerritt's stockings are selling very well. Perhaps he can contribute more. As for weavers and spinners, they are mostly doing it in their spare time, so that can't really be depended on to bring in much more. What was the next in your list? Oh yes, blacksmith shop. They are hard-pressed to keep the wagon factory supplied with metal parts and do the extra small things they can sell separately, but we can look at that more carefully. Maybe we can add something else, if we add another person or two as helpers. What about you, Benjamin, would you like to apprentice as a blacksmith? You would learn from some very good men." Benjamin hadn't thought too much about his future career, but this sounded not too bad, so he nodded almost eagerly.

"What about opening a store with an attached bakery and meat market?" Dorcas wondered.

"That sounds the most interesting. I think I will talk to George about it, and see what we can do in that department," replied Jacob thoughtfully. "I think it may be a very good suggestion. Thank you, Dorcas, you have come up with many good suggestions tonight. Has your new condition made you that much sharper than before?" His eyes brightened as he looked lovingly at his delightful wife.

"We have to get the gardens ready very soon, so that we will have lots of things to eat this coming winter, and perhaps we can plant enough that we could also sell fresh produce to the people in town," Dorcas's mind was tumbling again. Her joy seemed to be boundless, as her mind flitted from one thing to another as a butterfly in a flower patch. "I hope it's a girl. We need another girl in this house. I would love to be able to sew pretty things for a baby girl, and to knit and crochet things for her, as well."

"Yes to both," Jacob laughed, and, because the boys had done the dishes, both went to get ready for bed.

Chapter 20

Jacob couldn't see as well as before. Words and figures were not as clear as they had been in his younger years, but he struggled on, trying to keep up with the reckoning that was part of his work and the reading that he needed to do, in order to prepare messages. It seemed as though he and Gerritt were sharing the pulpit alternately now, so he was forced to keep studying, in order to provide the congregation with fresh spiritual challenges. Although he tried using a magnifying glass between his eyes and the words, his eyes began to ache from the strain.

One day after church, Martina, who was wearing small round spectacles, saw his bloodshot eyes and commented to him, "You need to see the new optician in Hamburg. He can fix you up with some glasses like these that I'm wearing that bring everything into proper focus for you."

Jacob was unaware of this new invention, but found out where the optician practiced and made a mental note to go there himself. The next day he went into Hamburg and paid the man a visit. The optician tried various lenses on each eye, finally coming up with the correct strengths. Because each eye was slightly different, the lenses needed to be individual, in order to compensate properly together. When he was done testing, he told Jacob to come back in a week, and he would have the lenses mounted in a frame that he could wear, so that the glasses would do their work for him at all times. When he went back a week later and had the frames adjusted to fit him properly, he was amazed that he could see as well as he had in his youth. Eye strain would no longer be a problem for him, no matter how much he read. Jacob mused at how Martina continued to feature in his life, even though she was no longer his wife. He wondered whether he looked as strange to others as Martina looked to him, with those tiny round lenses against that large square face. He was anxious to look into a mirror to see how he now appeared. The optician obliged him by bringing a looking glass for him, so that he could get used to what was now to be his personal image.

Jacob wasn't sure whether it was his new spectacles or just the good fortune of the Mennonites, but the extra money for the recruitment tax was coming in. In return, the Count gave them more freedom to enter other trades and to open new shops. The bakery-butcher shop-store was quickly taking shape. Mennonite brick layers and carpenters, some of which were Jacob's cousins, were constructing a building along one of the busy streets where Altona blended into Hamburg, where customers from both locations could buy their necessities in one place. One of the Mennonite men took on duties as butcher and another as baker, and George Janzen, grandson of the original Janzen who had run the store in Bad Oldesloe, became the store manager in Altona. Soon business was humming, as people came first out of curiosity, then out of loyalty, to the new outlet. *This might prove to be as big a help to the Mennonite coffers as the wagon factory or the brewery are,* Jacob reasoned. *Thank you, Dorcas, for the idea,* he breathed.

Spring work slowly rolled into summer work, and then harvest time came. The fields and gardens had yielded well. The efforts of many had paid off with abundance for the coming winter. Dorcas, who became larger and larger almost daily, as her due date was nearing, did what she could in the way of preparing for winter, but her greatest contribution in this was in the training of Mary, Susan and Elizabeth, who now had to take on a greater role in helping with the chores that sustained a normal household.

Jacob remembered that he had heard of his grandparents being involved in a Thanksgiving Festival in Bad Oldesloe. Somehow the tradition had gotten lost in the shuffle, as the families had been forced to flee Wuestenfelde to Altona, but he brought up the idea to the community elders, who approved heartily. Soon the town was abuzz with activity and planning committees. The day arrived, and with appropriate noise and ceremony, it went off well. The Mennonite community was indeed thankful for having been spared, as their village was totally destroyed, and they rejoiced in the privileges they had been granted by the Count. In fact, the Count and his family had been invited to share in the festivities and to give a greeting to his entire populace. Even the leaders of the village and some people from Hamburg enjoyed the events that were offered. God had supplied over and above all they could ask our think, so everyone was deeply thankful.

Christmas Day was approaching fast, and with it, Dorcas's due date. The family looked forward with gleeful anticipation to the coming blessing, and Jacob could not help but smile in triumphant pride, as he anticipated the addition to his tribe. The girls were taking on more and more of the day-to-day routines of cooking, cleaning and laundry – hard work for young bodies and developing minds – but they seemed to thrive on it, as they shared in the anticipation of the blessed event. Christmas Eve came, and with it came labor pains. Martina came again, to act as midwife. Everything went amazingly well for a mature woman delivering her first time. Then, as if by magic, out from the bedroom came the midwife, with two bundles tucked into her ample arms, smiling as broadly as her large face and small crooked mouth could.

"One boy and one girl," she announced to the waiting group in the main room. Everyone wanted to be first to hold the little ones, but Jacob took matters into his own hands, and he held each one, before giving it to the oldest, who was told to pass it down to the next younger one. Having made acquaintance with their new brother and sister, the children began to ask what they would be named.

"Your mother and I will have to discuss that, because we didn't pick any names yet. Do any of you have suggestions?"

"How about Jacob for the boy?" asked Willy.

"We already have a Jacob, because that is what JJ's full name is," replied Jacob smiling.

"How about Heinrich, for Mama's father?" asked Mary.

"Now that's a good idea, Mary. Thank you for that. Thank you, also, others, for thinking of good names," Jacob encouraged. "We could name the girl Leah for Mama's mother, or Heidi, for my mother."

"Yes, we like those ideas," the children chorused.

"How about Heidi Leah, for both grandmothers, and Heinrich Jacob for both grandfathers?" asked Benjamin.

"Now, I will take those ideas to your Mama, and we'll talk about them together. I think I will go in to see her now. Can I have the babies, please? By now they will probably be wanting a taste of their mother," Jacob said with a broad smile, taking the two bundles in his arms to follow Martina into the bedroom, where Dorcas was waiting patiently for him and the babies.

Christmas Eve, which is traditionally the time when German families celebrate Christmas together, proved to be the most blessed event that year, as Jacob and his family were able to celebrate not just the birth of Christ, but also the birth of two lovely, healthy children to Dorcas. The older children remembered all the old traditions they had grown up with, and they led in taking care of each detail. With a few trips into the bedroom to ask Dorcas for instructions, they were able to prepare the meal almost to perfection, and the whole family including Dorcas, were able to sit down together and rejoice in God's rich blessings. Even Martina was asked to stay to celebrate with them, which she accepted graciously. Gerritt and Lizzy were busy with some friends of theirs anyway, so she felt free to stay. A chorus of new cries from the bedroom suddenly announced that the new additions were ready to join the rest of the family, so Dorcas and Jacob went to get them. Soon they emerged, each carrying one.

"Here are Heinrich Jacob and Heidi Leah," Dorcas announced happily, "Can you tell which one is which?"

The children tried, but they were not very successful, for the features on the newly-born babies were not yet too well defined. Dorcas allowed them time to figure out which was which, and then she pointed out subtle differences that defined the one from the other. Soon everyone was able to tell who was who, and the evening passed with jovial mirth, as one after another held a little bundle in his or her arms and cooed soothingly to still their squalls.

"Father, I heard that at the first Christmas in Wuestenfelde, when Great Grandpa and Grandma came from Holland, that he told your father and his brothers and sisters about how they had come to live in Wuestenfelde," said Joshua. "Can you tell us that story tonight?"

"I would be happy to do that," Jacob replied. "But, they did it with a cup of mulled wine in their hands. Girls, did you get the spices out and warm up the wine?"

"Yes, we did, just like Mama told us to," said Susan.

"Well, let's see you pour us each a cup without spilling any," said Jacob, continuing in his fatherly role, even though they were in a celebratory mood. *Perhaps it is because we are all in a celebratory mood,* Jacob reasoned.

The necessary drink having been prepared and served, Jacob gathered the family together and began to tell them about the persecutions when his grandparents had converted to Anabaptism. He told about their going to Muenster and of the debacle there, and how his grandparents had fled before it was too late. He told about their wanderings along the lower Rhine and back to Friesland, and then of Baron von Ahlefeld's invitation for the followers of Menno Simon to come to his Fresenburg Estate, and how he had sustained them through those first few years. He told of the surprise wedding of his father and mother, and of Dorcas's father and mother, and of the events that led up to this.

Then he went on to tell them of his parents' lives, as their generation took over the reins of faith from their parents, and how their life had been so much better at Wuestenfelde, where the Mennonites had made their home for nearly a century, before they had been forced to flee when the Catholic armies of Tilly and Wallenstein descended on Wuestenfelde. He concluded with their triumphs and defeats in the few years at Altona, and told how the armies had finally signed peace agreements that stopped the carnage in their area. By this time, the wine cups were empty and the eyes were getting sleepy, so Jacob announced that they were going to open gifts. At that, every eye suddenly had new life, and a cheer went up.

Jacob called on Benjamin to come with him, and they disappeared into the shed behind the house. Soon they came in with arms full of carefully-wrapped bundles. Each one had a name on it, and as they called them out, each one came to get the present that had been picked out for them. Soon there was a general mess of paper scattered around the floor, as each one ripped off the wrappings to see what had been brought for them. Toys needed to be played with. Clothing items needed to be tried on, and useful things for school were tried out by others. No one seemed to want to hear Jacob's insistent call for bedtime, until he finally shooed the whole troop off to their rooms. Then he looked at Martina and asked whether he could drive her home. She accepted graciously, saying she had never experienced such a delightful birth before. She carefully avoided mentioning anything about the previous time she had been called to the Derksen household, for that was not a pleasant moment, either for her or for Jacob. Jacob went out and harnessed the horse and brought the carriage out for her, and off they went into Hamburg.

Dorcas, meanwhile, had nursed the babies and tucked them into their boxes, which served as cribs. Feeling very tired, now that her important work for this day was done and the children in bed, but realizing that the babies would be awake at various times throughout the night, she lay down on her bed and slept the sleep of the exhausted.

Chapter 21

Spring was approaching, as it had the year before, and Jacob wanted to know whether he could take his group of volunteers to Heubuden. The Count refused to answer their inquiries, and they didn't dare leave without his permission, for that would elicit another tax upon them all. The Mennonite council decided that it would be most prudent to go ahead with the spring planting, as if they would not be going. At least that way, if they had to stay, they would have sustenance for the coming winter. If they were given permission to go, it might come at an inappropriate time, such as planting or harvest, when they would have to remain anyway. Jacob chafed under this uncertainty, for he had spent many days planning each detail of their move and their resettling, and now the wagons with the equipment loaded on them were simply standing under their tarpaulin coverings. Sometimes Jacob wondered whether wagons, too, were disappointed in their lack of productive activity.

There was plenty to occupy Jacob's time. The wagon factory had gained several other products, and had been renamed Mennonite Manufacturing, for it produced iron farming implements and household goods in its blacksmith shop, and a variety of wooden goods in its carpentry shop, as well as having large areas for assembling the various things. Jacob enjoyed his role as supervisor of the manufacturing plant and pastor. He had once again taken on the role of the main preacher, and was affectionately called pastor by the entire congregation. Gerritt still preached fairly regularly, but his studies and his hosiery business were going well, and he couldn't spare the time to do more.

Dorcas and the children thrived together. Her gentle but instructive spirit caused each one to be drawn to her. When they got hurt in their playing, she was able to take the time with the suffering ones and comfort them, sometimes even causing them to laugh at their own painful experiences. Jacob could depend on her, no matter what. They seemed to have an uncanny understanding of each other. Perhaps that came because of their near relationship through their parents; perhaps it was just because God had meant them for each other. Jacob certainly thought so, and he believed sincerely that Dorcas felt the same. The babies grew stronger each day under her watchful, nurturing eye, and the other children loved them deeply, so they were often seemingly smothered with loving attention.

Seeding was finished. The gardens were tilled, planted and cared for. Calves and piglets had been born, and chicks, ducklings and goslings hatched. The whaling fleet, now made up of three ships, sailed out of the harbor. Summer weight cloth was selling well. Silk and linen were especially popular with the folks from Hamburg. Wagons and other goods from Mennonite Manufacturing commanded a good price. The store was a great success, with both the bakery and the butcher shop anchoring its sales to the populace of Altona and Hamburg. Still, there was no word from the Count.

Summer passed by, with haying occupying many of the men, and the gardens keeping the women busy. When they were not gathering the produce from the gardens, the young women were busy in the spinning room, which had been opened the winter before, producing the fine thread that made their cloth so special. The spinning room was also the place where socialization was actively cultivated. It was because of such rooms that young unmarried women came to be called spinsters. There were times when young men would come to sit idly by and watch the women spinning; the suspicion always was that that they were watching really one of the young women special to them. General socialization often turned to more specific socialization, as the looking began to be reciprocated by sly glances from the chosen one.

Church life took on a bit more of a regular nature. Since they were not molested, as they had been before, the Mennonites were able to begin singing once more. This also provided opportunity for more socialization, as special services were sometimes called to teach the congregation the songs that they had not been able to sing for some time. Being able to express themselves in the words and melodies of these grand hymns was a tonic for the beleaguered souls, who had dwelt mainly on their losses during the previous few years, since having had to move from Wuestenfelde or Friesland to Altona. Although they were in Germany, they still maintained the Dutch language for their worship services and hymns, while adapting to the local dialect for their daily speech. The feeling of the elders was that only if they kept up the mother tongue would they keep up the other traditions and beliefs that were so dear to them. God's people were, after all, to be a separate and peculiar people, so anything that would set them off from the world around was seen as valuable and was incorporated into their traditions and teachings.

Being different did not necessarily mean that they could not have social interaction with one another They staged a church picnic during the summer, when the weather was favorable and the work was not so arduous. As at other such social events, this provided a time when the men and women could catch up with one another, especially with distant relatives, on their lives and families. It also provided a time when young people could survey the available choices for future partners, similarly to what had brought their parents and grandparents together in years gone by. By now Gerritt and Suzie were recognized as a couple, much to the wonderment of the strict ones in the congregation, for in their minds, she had been defiled and could never hope to have a family of her own. Gerritt was seen by these as being dangerously close to having to be excommunicated from the church, though he was one of their regular preachers. Only his gentle, non-judgmental nature kept him from being accused in that way, for all recognized in the young man a model of what it meant to be a true Christian, and thus a true Mennonite. The majority of the Mennonites saw that trait in him and prevented the hot-headed, die-hard legalists from having their say. That did not prevent these legalists, though, from sitting together at the picnic, so that they could adequately express their disdain for such frivolous acceptance of one whom they deemed fallen.

Summer moved into autumn, when the work was once more multiplied on all fronts. Garden produce needed to be gathered in and prepared for storage; the various grains had to be mowed as they matured and set up in shocks, to be dried for threshing. The time-honored ways of threshing were still in use, so oxen were walked in a circle on the threshing floor dragging a sledge and to trample out the grain from the hulls. The remainder was then flailed with wooden tools until all the grain was on the floor. This was, after the straw had been raked away, carefully swept up and put into containers, from which it was winnowed in the wind. When it was all clean, it was put into bags for storage in the granaries. From there it would find its way to the mill for flour. The Mennonites had even been able to establish a mill with a windmill to drive it, so they were no longer dependent on the Germans to mill their grain. The straw, depending on which kind of grain it came from, was kept either for bedding or for fodder for the cattle and horses.

Fruit was gathered, pitted and cut into slices for drying, which was the only way of preserving this valuable commodity. Once dry, it would keep indefinitely in crocks or jars with lids. Many a delicious dessert would come out of these stores, or find its way into Pluma Moos, which was often eaten as a Faspa delicacy.

Once again, butchering day brought families together in the wagon factory, where they were able to process many hogs. It was, as usual, the busiest day of the year, but it also provided great opportunities for casual banter and gossip, as men and women who seldom worked together were in close proximity for the entire day. Once the sausages and bacon had been smoked and the hams laid in brine, everything was cleaned up in preparation for the next day's manufacturing.

George Toews went to the Count to see whether he would let the group depart for Prussia, but that leader continued to play games with the Mennonites, in threatening to charge more taxes or higher fees for services to them. It was clear to all that he was using the outmoded vagaries of serfdom to keep his cash flow strong. There was really no serfdom any more, but the leftover power to tax and to charge money from subjects was still practiced by all the nobles. George and Jacob sat and discussed the problems this caused. They felt that their situation, as it compared with that of Mennonites in Holland and other parts of Germany, was not really that intolerable. They had been given the freedom to work in whatever areas they wished, and they could come up with the atrocious sums of money extorted from them by the Count, as well as to provide a decent living for everyone in their group. Therefore, they decided not to pursue going to Heubuden, at least not for the foreseeable future.

This allowed Jacob to settle down to the daily work of running Mennonite Manufacturing and preaching when his turn came. The things that had been put in storage for taking along were now assembled into useful things, allowing for new industries to be started. Another brewery, this time for profit, was built. Shipping was another industry that had promise, so river freighters were rented or bought. Some of the men from Holland had experience in running such ships, so they were put in charge of them. The added industry allowed the people from the Lowlands to integrate into the Mennonite society more quickly, as they were no longer simply looking for subsistence, but could contribute positively to the industries that had been promoted.

Jacob was not expecting it, but one day the Elder arrived and asked for a meeting with the Council. His reason for coming, it turned out, was that he wanted to nominate Jacob as an Elder in the Mennonite Church. The Council discussed this, and agreed that he would make a very good Elder. This would mean, however, that he would have to travel to other congregations on a regular basis, so he would not be home as much. The Mennonites generally practiced a sort of lot system in choosing ministers, and refusal to take on the role could result in expulsion from the church. Because it was obvious to all in Altona that Jacob and Gerritt were the gifted preachers, the "lot" had fallen easily on them. It had now fallen on Jacob again, this time for greater responsibility, and possibly, greater danger. When the German clerics saw that one of the Mennonites was selected to hold this office, it awoke in them a special desire to persecute and hinder this person's work.

"I will pray about this," said Jacob humbly, "and I will let you know tomorrow." The Elder and the Council members agreed to allow him this time, and everyone went home.

"I have been asked to become an Elder in the Mennonite Church," began Jacob that evening at the supper table.

"It's about time," said Dorcas, surprising Jacob and everyone else with her vociferous endorsement.

"Why do you think that?" asked Jacob, incredulously.

"You have taken on the responsibility of being the local Elder for a long time, and everyone recognizes you for that, so it is time that you actually hold that title, not just the work," again Dorcas amazed Jacob with her insight into him and into the community situation.

"So you think I should accept the position?" Jacob wanted to be sure she was in agreement with him, if he took on the added responsibility.

"Of course, I don't see how you could refuse it, since you are doing everything an Elder does now, except for traveling to other congregations," said Dorcas matter-of-factly.

"Even if it means that I have to travel a good part of the time, and even if someone else has to take charge of Mennonite Manufacturing?" Jacob wanted to be certain that all the implications of this decision were understood by his wife and confidant.

"Yes, I believe God has called you to be an Elder, so go ahead and be an Elder," Dorcas encouraged.

"What do you think, Benjamin and you others," Jacob looked around the table at each of the children in turn. The older ones were beginning to look quite adult, he thought.

"We agree with Mother," said one after the other.

"All right, then, I will accept the position. It might mean that we will have to work with less income, as the Elder is not paid, except in occasional gifts from churches he visits. It will also mean that I have to deal with the problems in churches all over northern Germany. I will have to become licensed to conduct weddings, baptisms and funerals. There is a lot of responsibility involved in being an Elder, instead of just a preacher." Jacob wanted everyone to understand how their life would change, once he took on this role, but he was encouraged by the expressions of agreement he saw in each of them. "I will go yet tonight to talk with the Elder, and tell him that we feel that God is calling me to this office and responsibility." With that, he put on his coat and hat and left the house.

The first item of business was to appoint someone else to manage Mennonite Manufacturing, and he suggested that the man who had stepped into the breach when he was ill was the right man for the job. All the workers were pleased to hear of Jacob's appointment, and they were genuinely accepting of the new boss, so work went on pretty much as usual.

"The Elder said that he had talked with George, and that they had agreed that my regular stipend from Mennonite Manufacturing will still come to me, to allow me the freedom to travel to other churches and assist them, without becoming a burden to them," Jacob told the crew at the plant. They all cheered and said that this was fair, making Jacob considerably relieved, for he had wondered how he would provide for his enlarged family without a paying job.

As he met with the Elder again, he was informed that he was to accompany him to the first church, where there was a problem to be worked out. Jacob prepared himself, taking a community horse and carriage, so as to leave some transportation with Dorcas and the children. The boys were quite familiar with harnessing and bridling their horse and hitching it to the carriage, so he had no worries about that. He also knew that Dorcas was eminently able to take things in stride, so that, too, was one worry he did not carry. He and the senior Elder left for the ailing church, where Jacob would be introduced to his new role as arbitrator.

Small Mennonite groups had settled throughout northern Germany and Holland, keeping in touch with each other through the traveling Elder and through businessmen that sought to sell the goods produced by each group. In some cases, the settlers were under the heel of a despotic lord, and in other cases, they had privileges accorded to them by a generous and tolerant ruler. In some cases, the hardships had produced difficulties in the congregations, as the limitations of the ruler came into conflict with the teachings and principles of the Mennonites. That accentuated the already strong feelings of some who were more legalistic in their interpretation of Menno's teachings. Because of isolation from other congregations, these disputes sometimes boiled over into church divisions, with one group refusing to have fellowship with those of the other group. It was just such a case that Jacob was now to visit. It was not without difficulty that the senior Elder and Jacob were able to talk to both groups and find out what the real issues were, and then to get the two groups together to discuss ways of dealing with them. At long length, they were able to extract a grudging agreement from the breakaway group to return to the main group. Some concessions had to be made on the part of the main group, however, and they were forced to take a much stricter stance toward those who did not dot their "i's" as the others did.

At this point the senior Elder went on his way, and left Jacob to continue the negotiations within this group, seeking to mend the fences that had gotten broken. As he probed further, he found that there was also a marriage problem that was festering within the group, and it had contributed to the strong stance of some, including the man involved. Jacob, having had some experience with marriages, was able to counsel the man and his estranged wife, and to bring about a measure of reconciliation. He was sure that this would have a very positive effect on the church situation, once the couple had worked out their difficulties, so he spent time with them, adding bits and pieces to the wisdom he had been able to bring to their situation.

Jacob returned to Altona thinking that God had helped him in his very first duty as an Elder. He was happy, however, to come back to his home and family, and he realized that, no matter how often he would have to travel away from home, he would always treasure returning to the comforts and love of his wife and family.

He went to the local Standesamt to register his new position, and to obtain the licenses to marry and to bury. The senior Elder had provided him with the appropriate forms. The following weeks were taken with planning his next circuit of church visits. It was common for the Elder to just arrive at any given church at any time, as his schedule allowed. Therefore, Jacob thought it would be good to visit all the churches in his new district, which lay to the north of Hamburg. He prepared some books of messages for untrained preachers, who had been conscripted by lot, to read when their turn came. This was often the most appreciated part of his duties, as the congregations were often comprised of Dutch immigrants who were losing command of their own language as they interacted with the German population around them. Still, the leaders in almost every congregation insisted on keeping the Dutch language for worship, claiming that this would keep their teachings and actions pure. The problem then surfaced that the men who had been selected by lot to serve as preachers couldn't read Dutch very well, thus making them basically unfit for their new calling. Another aspect of his job was to distribute gifts and donations from other churches that were experiencing economic success to those who were not. Altona, instead of being a receiving church, as it had been for the first few years, was now able to share with others that were in desperate straits. Jacob especially enjoyed this part of his role as Elder, for the expressions of thankfulness and relief were palpable. He could report back to his home church of the joy their gift had brought to those who felt forsaken.

The Count had also been busy. He wanted to talk to George and Jacob, so they went to visit him at his manor. As they went in, the lord met them cordially and showed them to the sumptuous parlor, where he bade them take seats in the comfortable chairs. He seemed to have something important to announce to them, so the men held their peace and waited until he had poured them each a glass of their own beer and was settled in his well-padded chair.

"I have something to discuss with you," the man began with a glint in his eye and the semblance of a smile on his face. George and Jacob took the cue and relaxed, for they had feared the worst.

"You don't have to be worried, I have good news for you," the Count continued, as though he was lecturing a group of minor officials. "We have discussed your request to leave for Prussia, and we have also discussed the taxes that have been levied on you Mennonites. I believe we can help you with one of those items, at least."

George and Jacob looked at one another, then at the Count. What did he have in mind? Was he now going to allow them to make their move? Jacob couldn't help wondering how that would play out with his new role as Elder.

"The war has moved southward, so we are not in need of training more soldiers at present. Therefore, we can reduce the recruitment tax that was imposed on you during the war years. I'm sure that will come as a welcome piece of information, as I have been informed that you have been chafing considerably under this load."

Now the two men looked at each other with a quizzical look in their eyes. Was this a new trick? What possessed the Count to take away a main form of income?

"You are probably wondering why I have decided to remit your recruitment tax," the Count observed. "I want you Mennonites to remain in Altona, so I am willing to make some concessions to you, in order to keep you here. I realize that some want to emigrate to Danzig, where you think you will have more freedom. I believe that, if I make the concession to drop the recruitment tax, you will have no reason to leave. Therefore, I am willing to take this burden from you, in order to make it as easy as possible to attract your group to remain here."

This was such a surprise to George and Jacob that they couldn't think of anything to say. Each took a sip from their glass to stall for time. To be sure, Jacob wondered when his group would ever be able to leave, but they had already conceded that it would not be any time soon, if ever. The Count had just sealed that. The extra income that had gone toward the recruitment tax could now be used to expand other businesses. That would be good for both Altona and the Mennonites, and ultimately for the Count. George and Jacob thanked the Count profusely for his generosity and accepted the prepared decree from him relieving the Mennonites of the tax burden.

A meeting of the Council was called as quickly as possible, and the news of the new decree was shared with the men. Long discussion ensued, in which a number of ideas were put forward for added industries or expansions of present ones. It was finally agreed that the money would become a trust fund, from which entrepreneurial Mennonites could borrow, in order to build private businesses. Since the group felt more secure now under the Count's leadership, they thought that the somewhat socialistic way in which they had run businesses before was no longer necessary. They would allow those with special gifts and ideas to try them out, with a very low interest loan.

"I am wondering how we can buy out Mennonite Manufacturing," thought Jacob out loud over the supper table. "The Count has relieved us of the recruitment tax, so we are taking that money and allowing people to borrow from it, in order to establish their own private businesses. Perhaps I should buy the industry I helped to build up. That would secure our income, while I do my duty as Elder."

"Oh, that seems like it would be far more than we could ever manage," Dorcas ejaculated questioningly. Ever the practical one, she couldn't imagine them having a debt to pay off. What if business isn't good enough? What if the whole thing burns down? What if the Count changes his mind, as he has done many times before? What if the war breaks out again?" There seemed to be no end of possible reasons why such a venture could fail, and Dorcas could survey all of them in the twinkling of an eye.

"I agree that it is a bit risky," said Jacob thoughtfully, "but I think it has some merit. The business has grown quite a bit, and our products sell very well from Holland to Prussia. That seems pretty secure to me. The money is available to anyone that wants to start a new business. Do you have any ideas for something else we could start?"

"Perhaps you could take over the things that relate to carpentry and allow the blacksmithing to go its own way," suggested the practical wife.

"Now, that is an idea worth thinking about," responded Jacob with new vigor in his voice and expression. "We could begin a shop to manufacture wagons, wooden casks for the breweries, household articles, cabinets and coffins. There will be more need for cabinets, once people begin to build their own homes here in Altona. And perhaps those who are now running the blacksmith shop will want to do the same with that part of the company."

Jacob talked with the other ones responsible for Mennonite Manufacturing, and mentioned the possibility of obtaining substantial money from the fund to make it possible to split the company into two parts and each of them could run their own part for their own profit. Naturally, there would still have to be a contribution to the general fund, out of which the Council provided for needy Mennonites, the elderly, and those who were ill, as well as for other congregations that faced special needs. All in all, the men thought it was a good idea, and they commissioned Jacob to ask for funds to make it possible for them to take over their shares of the company. It was only at that point that Jacob suddenly realized that he would be traveling most of the time, so he would not be able to manage the shop himself, anyway, just as he wasn't managing it now. That would have to wait, and he would see whether the present manager would continue under him, rather than under the Council, as at present. Those in charge of the blacksmith shop were well able to manage their business themselves, so that would not be a problem.

Jacob presented his idea to the Council, and they nearly gasped at his audacity. In the end, though, after due consideration of the many requests for funding, the Council offered him a considerable sum, divided over the next year, as it came in. They would allow him to pay that amount to the Council in return for assuming ownership of just over half the company. Jacob would be responsible for finding his own location for the new enterprise, as the original building was designed to be a blacksmith shop. The town of Altona was happy to keep the shop running, so using the building was no problem to them. It would have to continue to serve as the meeting place for both Jews and Mennonites, as well, for they were still not allowed to build their own building for worship.

Jacob went home with divided heart. On the one hand, he accepted the fact that the Council had decided on things the way they had. On the other hand, he wondered how he was going to find a place to carry on the manufacturing of wagons and the other things he planned. He went home to discuss things with the one who always seemed to have an answer for every problem he encountered.

Chapter 22

"I want to . . ." Jacob began at the supper table.

"I have an idea," Dorcas broke in, "you could go to the cabinet shop where you used to work and ask to buy them out. Then you would have a place to manufacture all the things you have been doing in the blacksmith shop."

Jacob sat there, stunned. How could Dorcas have known about the problem he had just encountered? As usual, she had a solution for every problem, so her suggestion didn't surprise him at all. He looked at her stupidly, shook his head, smiled a perplexed smile, nodded, and attacked his soup with an energy he had not thought possible.

"Well, I knew you would need a place to work, if you took over part of Mennonite Manufacturing, and I knew the blacksmith crew would want to keep the present shop for their work, since it is set up for that anyway. I just thought that the other shop would be a solution." Dorcas seemed as matter-of-fact as always, and, as usual, her solution was practical and purposeful.

"After our meeting of the Council, I began to wonder how we could make this whole thing work. It seemed to me to be much bigger than

I had thought. But you make it all seem so easy," Jacob began to come out of his stupor.

"Well, you always get yourself into these overwhelming situations, so somebody has to look out for you," Dorcas laughed.

"Thank you very much, Dorcas, I agree, you certainly have a knack for bailing me out of difficulties. And your ideas are always so practical and workable. I will go over to the shop tomorrow and see whether your plan would work. It is certainly big enough to handle our operation, including the wagon building, and it has the equipment we would need to manufacture the other things we plan to make."

Supper took on a new spirit. Jacob became jovial instead of introverted, and everyone took a signal from that to lighten their conversation with each other. The evening went by quickly, as Benjamin suggested that they play a table game as a family. Everyone joined in on a game of Morris, which is a bit like the modern tick-tack-toe, where you have to get three pieces in a row, but is played on a prepared board with markers. Dorcas remembered that she had baked an Obstplautz, and she warmed some milk and added some syrup that she had gotten from a Jewish merchant, who said it was a drink of the gods in America, made from a bean-like nut called cacao. Everyone joined in heartily, as they took their portions of hot chocolate and a fruit streusel. Bedtime was happy for everyone that night.

Jacob returned from his visit to the carpentry shop to report to Dorcas what he had found out. Over lunch they discussed the terms of sale that had been negotiated. As it happened, the owner was considering selling the shop anyway, as he was getting too old to carry on the work himself, and it was costing him too much to keep skilled workers. Mennonite Manufacturing had cut into his profits, as their products seemed to sell better than his, and he was not strong enough to handle the competition any more. He was quite happy to negotiate good terms with Jacob for the sale.

"Now, all we have to do is to get the necessary funds from the Council to buy both our part of Mennonite Manufacturing and also the carpentry shop. Then we have to move everything over to the carpentry shop. This won't be easy, because we are moving from Holstein to Hamburg, so we'll have to get a new trade license here." Jacob's mind was going faster than it had gone in months, as he contemplated the details of what lay ahead.

"You will succeed, I know," Dorcas assured him, as they ate their noon meal together. This was not something that they could do very often, so they treasured this time together. Jacob felt strong in the glow of his wife's admiring encouragement. She, in turn, felt secure and comfortable with this man that God had brought into her life. The waking babies only increased her joy.

"I must get busy with the rest of the plan. Thank you for such a fine dinner," Jacob excused himself and left the house.

George was interested in Jacob's ambitious plan. It seemed to have all the makings of being solid financially and practically. He did not see any problems in presenting facts and figures to the Council for approval of the loan, which would be paid out of funds no longer paid out of brewery profits. Others, including himself, had also presented plans to borrow from this fund, so it might be difficult for everyone to get the required amounts. The Council would have to decide that evening.

At that moment, a man stumbled into the room, road-weary and tired. He introduced himself as a Mennonite preacher from a village north of Altona, and he wanted to talk to the Elder. Jacob took him aside, asking him whether he had eaten or needed something to drink. The man said he had not eaten since the evening before nor drunk anything. Jacob suggested that he come home with him, as there was still food left over from the delicious meal Dorcas had served him just an hour ago. The man thankfully accepted the kind invitation and left with his Elder.

As the man ate, Jacob and Dorcas listened to his tale. Apparently one of the preachers in his congregation had been discovered to be guilty of incest with his teenage daughter, and now she was pregnant. The church had asked this preacher to come and seek help from the

Elder. Jacob and Dorcas looked at each other in amazement and sadness. How could anyone do such a thing? Jacob thought about how he should be involved. He contemplated how his counselling would go, if he left with the man. He wondered what was happening in the guilty man's family at this moment and in the Mennonite church in the remote village. He decided that what was done was done, he could not change that. He would attend the evening meeting of the Council and present his plea for the loan, which would also seal the deal concerning Mennonite Manufacturing; he would then conclude the deal with the owner of the carpentry shop the next morning. That would get things started towards amalgamating the two businesses into one. His foreman, Dave, would know what to move over and how to set it up, so he would leave him in charge of the move, while he left in the afternoon with the preacher. Dorcas agreed that this would work best for everyone concerned.

Negotiations went well that evening, the deal was concluded, the money was made available. The preacher stayed with Jacob and Dorcas that night and enjoyed visiting other Mennonites during the morning, as Jacob continued his business dealings. They, too, went well, and just before lunch, he was able to make the arrangements with Dave to move his equipment to the new location. He then made arrangements to have a community horse and carriage made ready for him to use, packed hurriedly, ate lunch at his house with the pastor and Dorcas, had prayer together with his family, and left for his new duties.

The church meeting, held in a large house that had been the meeting place for the small congregation, was not pleasant. As details of the situation unfolded, the unseemliness of it hung over the small group of believers. The man and his daughter that were involved were not present, but his wife, the mother of the girl, was there, weeping in agony as detail after detail was exposed. Her shame was almost overwhelming, as she felt that somehow she must have been at fault somewhere along the line, even though she had been totally unaware of what had happened, until her fourteen-year-old daughter had obviously become pregnant. It was then that she informed the other preacher that had come to Jacob for help. Strangely, the disgraced preacher's name was also Jacob. The congregation waited expectantly for the Elder's decision.

"Jacob must be excommunicated from the Mennonite Church," the Elder Jacob began. "He has disgraced the beliefs of our church, and he has not deported himself in a way that Mennonite preachers are expected to act. We must report his excommunication to the local magistrates. When one is excommunicated from the Mennonite Church, he is no longer able to claim the privileges that our rulers have accorded us, so he will probably be required to join the military and serve his required term there. It will definitely have an impact on the rest of the family, who are innocent. For that we cannot do anything, except to help Gertrude and her children in every way possible. I suggest that we take your daughter back to Altona with us, where either my wife and I, or someone else from the congregation, will look after her and help with her pregnancy and the birth. In that way, she will not be forced to endure the stares of the local group here, and she will be able to begin a new life for herself there. Is the local congregation able to care for the rest of the family?"

Everyone agreed that this was the best way to deal with the situation, and to help out the family. Service in the army would be an appropriate punishment for the offender, and the family would be looked after in the best possible way. Jacob agreed to accompany the other preacher to the Standesamt to take care of the excommunication, and then a communal meal was eaten by the entire group.

The next day, after the men had taken care of the business and had seen the magistrates come to induct the offending Jacob into the army, Jacob the Elder spent time with the new "widow," to comfort her. He was able to help with the arrangements for Katherine to accompany him to Altona. Jacob agreed to preach that evening, and he chose as his text Galatians 6:1-10, where the congregation was encouraged to "bear one another's burdens," and to "not be weary in well doing, for in due season we shall reap, if we faint not."

Jacob left with Katherine after breakfast the next morning. Although she was not very communicative, Jacob was able with his humor and good sense to draw her out. By the time they reached his house, she was fairly responsive. Dorcas's welcome totally disarmed her, and she responded immediately to the natural radiance that came from this motherly woman. After a good meal with the family, Katherine was shown to the makeshift quarters that the house could offer her. She was able to have warm water and towels, with which she could bathe herself, and then she settled down for a good sleep in the strange new household.

"I think we should ask Martina to care for Katherine," Dorcas said out of the blue, once the girl had gone to her quarters. "She would be able to handle it well, and she could help her with the birth, when her time comes."

"Now that is a novel idea," Jacob was getting used to saying this to Dorcas, but this time, it was actually something especially unique, even for Dorcas. She usually saw herself as the solution to every problem, and Jacob had expected her to see it as her own duty to look after the woeful waif. Her willingness to second this responsibility to Martina, of all people, seemed out of character.

"I thought about it quite a bit while you were gone," Dorcas continued, "and I think it would be good for both Martina and Katherine. Martina dealt with the situation of Gerritt taking a liking to Suzie very well, and I believe she has room for another person. I'll be glad to ask her, if you agree."

"It does seem to be a good solution, and we certainly don't have room to keep her for long. Yes, I would like you to ask Martina to look after her." Jacob was constantly amazed at how Dorcas fitted in with his various schemes and responsibilities. God had certainly made no mistake in giving her to him in his hour of need, and He was proving it daily, as one thing after another unfolded in his life. They took care of the last things of the day and got ready for bed.

Jacob found that Dave had gotten most of the equipment moved from Altona to Hamburg, and he was pleased at how well the additional machinery fitted into the new shop. The workers that had been part of his wagon building industry, as well as those who were manufacturing other household items and cabinets were willing to come with him to the new facility, and the two carpenters that were left in the shop he had bought were also willing to work for him, so he was well served with good workers. They were already beginning to prepare parts for assembly of wagons once again.

George had some new information for him when he went to see him. The whaling crew had come in with an exceptional catch. Their oil sales would sustain the fund for all the loans that were being processed, and the men could buy their boats now, so that they would also become independent contractors. God was looking after the Mennonites in an abundant way, for which both men were deeply thankful.

"Martina will be happy to look after Katherine," Dorcas beamed as Jacob came into the house.

"And the whaling crew has come in with a record catch, so that our fund is going to be able to handle all the private loans that have been asked for, allowing us all to buy our businesses and become independent." Jacob beamed in return. "God is certainly looking after us. It has taken a long time, and it has been very difficult at times to meet the demands of the Count. Maybe he was feeling guilty for taking advantage of us."

"And Katherine will get the best of care and the best of love under Martina's eye," added Dorcas.

"Then we better get supper on the table and tell her about her new future," said Jacob with a grin.

Supper was a happy occasion. Katherine was deeply thankful for Dorcas's motherly care, and she trusted her judgment regarding a permanent place for her and her coming baby. The rest of the family was equally happy for her, for by now the older ones had guessed why she was with them. Being almost as old as Benjamin and a year older than

Joshua, she seemed to fit right into the family. They discussed openly with her what would be involved in moving into the heart of Hamburg. That would happen the next day, Dorcas said. Since the children were mostly in school, and Benjamin would be at work, she would be able to accompany her into the city to Martina's place. Martina would be able to take time off work to get her settled in. The rest of the evening was spent in happy reverie, with another few rounds of Morris and hot chocolate keeping everyone's wits sharp.

Dorcas gathered the things that Katherine had brought with her, added a few from her own store of hand-me-downs that the girl could use, bundled her babies and JJ into the carriage, harnessed the horse and hitched it to the shafts and got in together with Katherine. Together they drove the busy streets into the heart of the largest city in northern Europe at the time. When they arrived at Martina's house, the big woman virtually beamed at Katherine, ushering her into her apartment, where she had a lovely room prepared for her. They all sat down while she served tea and some bought German Kuchen, and they all chatted cheerily for an hour. Then Dorcas said that she really must be getting back to the house, so that she would be there when the children arrived home from school, and so that she could get supper ready for her family.

"Good-bye, Katherine, I'm sure that Martina will look after you very well. She knows our family very well, and is almost a part of it, so you won't ever be far from us," Dorcas assured her. Off she went with her little entourage to navigate the streets of the big city back to her house.

Chapter 23

Jacob got his new shop running smoothly over the next few days, and in the meantime, he was preparing things to take along with him on his first circuit as Elder. Sermon books would be needed, so he commissioned a printer to print up a number of copies of his collected sermons. He had gotten several copies of sermons by Dirk and Obbe Philips, as well, which were always much appreciated by the lay preachers that served most of the churches. He would need forms to submit at the various Standesämter, when he would perform weddings or funerals, or when some other situation called for reporting to the officials of the village or town that he visited. Mennonites were barely tolerated; they were not recognized as an official church, but as a sect that needed to be watched all the time, in case of strange behaviors or teachings. The debacle at Muenster in the previous century had set the whole theological world on edge, and the Mennonites, as the afterglow of the Anabaptist movement that generated that chaotic situation, could not shake the negative image that this incident had provoked. Jacob recognized this, and he also carried many tracts that had been written by Menno Simon, refuting this form of religious zeal as being unbiblical. He thought of writing on his own, but realized that he didn't really have time to do more, so he contented himself with sharing his sermons with inexperienced men.

The Lutheran Church was also moved greatly by the Muenster incident. The chief theologians wrote strong diatribes against the teachings of the Anabaptists, using this incident as an example of what happens when untrained minds get hold of God's Word and wrest it to their own ends. Some Pfarrer, or pastors, however, began to think that there was something to the doctrine of the inner voice of the Holy Spirit that transformed the life of the individual believer, and not just the politics of church life. Perhaps this came about as a result of their observing the way in which the Mennonites considered their relationship to the teachings of the Bible on salvation, church membership and daily life with God. Pietism may have had its beginnings in this desire for a deeper walk with God, which was driven by the vicissitudes of the 30-Years War around them.

During this time the congregation celebrated Harvest Festival. Shades of the original one in Bad Oldesloe, at which the Baron had provided so much in the way of spirit and entertainment, were again visible, as the Altona Buergermeister had brought in some musicians, jugglers and clowns to entertain the people. The Count did an admirable job of welcoming the village and praising the Mennonites for their diligence and good morals. Again the women prepared savory and sweet dishes for everyone to sample, and the people of Altona could be seen testing the various dishes with relish. Even some of the Jews came to celebrate this thanksgiving to God for the harvest, saying that it was like one of their festivals, only celebrated less liturgically. It brought a sense of unity and camaraderie to the group that had shared so many trials together.

When everything was in order, Jacob decided that the time had come for him to make his first round of churches. It was early November, a time when most of northern Germany is covered in mists and fog, and the cold winds are beginning to blow in from the North Sea. He was glad that his carriage had a good roof and some canvas sides that could be tied down. Even the front could be sealed up against the wind and rain, with only slots for the reins. Some bricks warmed in the fireplace were also brought along, to keep him warm on the journey. After many hugs and kisses, he bade his family good-bye and headed north to the place where he had gone for Katherine first.

Things had settled down quite a bit in the congregation. Jacob the Offender had gone off to take military training, leaving his wife and other children in the care of the Church Council. They were doing the best they could to support her and care for her physical, spiritual and emotional needs, though the latter was proving to be quite a chore. She had loved her husband and had trusted him, and he had actually been quite good to her, so she missed him terribly. She also missed her eldest daughter very much. Jacob was able to describe to her how they had been able to provide for Katherine, and this gave her mother a tremendous boost in morale. He was also able to give the church leaders a gift from the Altona congregation, to help them look after the stricken family. Jacob preached one evening and met with the Council to discuss further issues. During this time he stayed with the preacher that had come to call for him, and he was able to encourage him in his work, leaving a book of his messages and several tracts. From there he went to the next congregation, and the next, until he had visited every church in his district. In some places he had the privilege of marrying couples that had been waiting for his arrival. In others, he assisted in burying one of the congregation's elder statesmen or women. The trip took four weeks, during which time he could not contact his family. By the time he returned home, it was time to begin Advent celebrations.

Christmas Eve was celebrated as a complete family. Martina and her children were invited to participate with the Derksens, and Katherine was also there, already showing her growing girth. She had attended church with Martina, Gerritt and Lizzy, so she knew people fairly well by this time. This brought a sense of relief to all, for she entered wholeheartedly into the games and gossip of the day. The meal, as usual was superb, with a roasted ham as the centerpiece, potatoes, gravy, cooked peas, and a cole slaw of red cabbage, apples and walnuts. Martina, who had continued to supervise the beekeepers, brought a jar of delicious honey. Mary had begun baking under her mother's watchful eye, and she presented a tasty dessert. Everyone praised her efforts. She had been well taught, and she had passed her big test with flying colors.

Gifts were exchanged all around, and the evening concluded with Jacob recounting once more their family history, beginning with Jacob and Eva, who had brought the family to Wuestenfelde, and continuing through his parents' generation to his and the children's. Every ear was tuned in, as this provided a sense of identity and meaning to their lives, as it had to his, when he had been a child in his parents' home. Jacob closed with a prayer of thanks for his family, for those that God had added to it, and for his new role as Elder, which he was enjoying. He praised God for the way that his new business was going, and that it was producing good quality goods, even when he had to be away. He was thankful for the Count's generosity and good will. Seemingly forgotten was the former desire to emigrate farther east to Prussia. God would look after that, too, as He had cared for all the other details of his busy life. God was good.

CPSIA information can be obtained
at www.ICGtesting.com
Printed in the USA
BVHW081628020222
627786BV00006B/224